The cougar's black-tipped ears lay flat against its head, its jaws parted in a snarl. Chiri reached it first and the cougar's talon-tipped paws ripped at him. The big dog dodged the strike. The cougar turned its attention to Link. Crouched low, lips bared and tail twitching, straight at Link it launched its tawny, spring-steel length . . .

Wild Trek
by Jim Kjelgaard
Author of *Big Red*

"A sure-fire hit . . . An exciting manhunt, a Crusoe-like struggle for survival, and a fine partnership between a man and his dog."   *—The New York Times*

"Full of thrills, WILD TREK holds the absorbed attention of readers who like outdoor adventure and animals."
     —Horn Book

"Superior adventure reading . . . Excellent, fast-paced action yarn reminiscent of the works of Jack London."
     —Kirkus

"Well-written story, conveying the majestic beauty of the Canadian wilderness, and the suspense and danger of a desperate struggle for survival."   *—School Library Journal*

Wild Trek
Jim Kjelgaard

A BANTAM SKYLARK BOOK®
TORONTO · NEW YORK · LONDON · SYDNEY · AUCKLAND

RL 6, 011-014

WILD TREK

*A Bantam Book / published by arrangement with
Holiday House, Inc.*

PRINTING HISTORY

*Holiday House edition published April 1950
10 printings through September 1970*

*Bantam Skylark edition / November 1981
2nd printing . . . . . . July 1983*

ISBN 0-553-15232-7

Published simultaneously in the United States and Canada

*Bantam Books are published by Bantam Books, Inc. Its trade-
mark, consisting of the words ''Bantam Books'' and the por-
trayal of a rooster, is Registered in U.S. Patent and Trademark
Office and in other countries. Marca Registrada. Bantam
Books, Inc., 666 Fifth Avenue, New York, New York 10103.*

PRINTED IN THE UNITED STATES OF AMERICA

CW   12 11 10 9 8 7 6 5

For
**ROBERTA
FORSYTH**

Contents

Wild Trek

1
Visitor

Chiri, the Snow Dog, had been hunting all night. An hour before dawn he found the trail of a snow-shoe rabbit, and spent half an hour running the rabbit down. He ate, and rested until the sun came up. Then he started back to Link Stevens' cabin on the Gander.

After a long and hard winter of near-starvation, spring had burst like a green bubble over the north country. Creeks spilled out of their banks, rivers roared toward their meeting with the arctic sea. The willow thickets sported a new cloak of fuzzy green buds and green grass showed in every clearing. The whiskeyjacks, who loved this north land so much that they shivered through its winter snows rather than leave for more temperate climates, shrieked their boundless joy because spring had come again.

Chiri slunk from the tangle of spruces where he had caught the rabbit, and paused at the edge of a meadow. An ordinary dog would have run heedless-

1

ly across the meadow, but Chiri was no ordinary dog. He had been born under a windfall near the wild Carney Meadows, and when he was only four months old had seen his mother and two brothers killed by a savage black wolf. Chiri alone had escaped, and for a year of his life had lived as a wolf does. Finally he had been caught by the trapper, Link Stevens, to whom he had gradually given his whole-hearted allegiance. Later, when Link had been waylaid by the black wolf's pack, Chiri had battled and killed the wolf, and returned to the Gander with Link and Lud, the only other dog in Link's pack to survive the wolves' attack.

The big dog, a blend of staghound and Husky, did not run heedlessly into the meadow because his instincts and impulses were still those of a wolf. He had fought alone for survival in a land where only the strongest lived, and he had won his fight. Now he could forget nothing that harsh experience had taught him. Chiri remained in the spruces, and turned to slink through them to a place where the wind brushed his nose more advantageously. He was not afraid, for he had never feared anything; he wished merely to know what lay ahead before he ventured any farther.

The wind brought him the scent of a feeding deer, and Chiri studied the odor thoroughly. Last fall, for some obscure reason, the Gander had become almost a wildlife desert. All the game had left, and getting anything at all to eat had been a desperate-enough battle. Now, with spring, the game was returning. However, since he had just fed, Chiri was not hungry enough to be interested in any deer.

A muted, far-off gabbling drifted out of the sky and Chiri turned his head toward the sound. The northbound geese that were winging toward distant nesting places were mere dots in the sky. Chiri turned away from the sound, not interested in geese, either. But he did feel the fierce joy, and the great awakening, that spring brought to the whole thawing land.

He broke into a trot, because now he missed Link and wanted to be back with him. For a way he followed a little stream which normally pursued a placid way through the spruces. Fed by melting snows, at this season the stream was bank-full and rippled by strong currents. Chiri walked onto a bit of land that jutted into the water, gathered himself, and sprang effortlessly to the other side. He trotted through the forest, snuffling here and there at rabbit or deer traces.

Chiri came to the Gander, which was now white water foaming between cut banks, and unhesitatingly plunged in. He swam to the north bank of the river, shook himself, and resumed his distance-devouring trot. Link Stevens' home cabin, a twelve by sixteen foot log structure, was only a little way away. Chiri knew even before he came to the cabin that Link had not yet returned. The big dog's ears drooped slightly and his tail sagged.

He broke over the last little rise and saw the cabin. It was built on a knoll in a clearing, far enough from the river so that even the fiercest flood waters never approached its doors. Near it was a storage shed and to one side, far enough apart so their chained occupants could not fight, were five dog houses. During the past winter each of those houses had had a tenant, but three of them had been killed by the black wolf's pack. Now only Lud emerged from a kennel and wagged a happy tail as Chiri approached.

Chiri went forward to sniff noses. Lud, a philosophical creature who would accept anything except loneliness, whined eagerly. Very early that morning, after tossing Lud a venison knuckle, Link had left the cabin to hunt. Lud had gnawed every shred of anything edible from the knuckle, but as Chiri came nearer he covered it with his body. It was a natural move for the gentlest trail dog will instinctively defend his food.

Chiri, however, paid no attention to it. He sniffed noses with Lud and trotted hopefully to the cabin. His ears drooped a bit more and his tail sagged lower; the only scents of Link were stale ones. Chiri wandered disconsolately back to Lud, who had been watching him worriedly. Having company at last, Lud was reluctant to lose it.

For a few minutes the dogs lay side by side, Lud entirely contented but Chiri increasingly anxious. He was not worried about Link, but he missed him. A wilderness rover in his own right, Chiri knew only, that after being away from his master, he always had a great yearning for his companionship and a hunger for his friendly caresses.

Chiri rose suddenly and ran back to the cabin door. Lud strained to the end of his chain, wagging a pleading tail and whining as he begged his companion to return. Chiri glanced at Lud, then sought Link's trail.

The scent was easily discernible to Chiri's half-wild nose. The big dog followed it around a corner of the cabin and up the slope. He heard Lud's protests at being again deserted, but Chiri did not look back. It was not for him to question why Lud must always be tied while he himself was always allowed to run free.

He could not know that, though he was a big and hardy dog, Lud still had only an orthodox dog's rearing. Packs of dog-hating timber wolves roamed the Gander, and Lud would stand no chance whatever should such a pack corner him. Chiri was well able to take care of himself, but above and beyond that there was Link's understanding of his wild training. Link had always dreamed of the ideal trail dog, a companion that would travel with him wherever he went and carry his own weight. He had found that dog in Chiri, but at the same time he had recognized the big dog's independent spirit and ability to fend for himself. Link never chained Chiri because he knew that no steel chain could ever bind such a dog to any man. Chiri would have to give himself, and the bonds of love that held him to Link were far more powerful than any shackles ever fashioned in a forge.

His nose still to the ground, Chiri followed Link's trail up the sloping ridge behind the cabin and into the spruces. He ran fast now, certain of himself and of the scent he pursued. Chiri stopped suddenly. A cross wind, playing low among the trees, brought him Link's fresh scent. Chiri stood still a moment, testing the wind and verifying the news it had brought him. Link was there, returning almost by the same route he had taken to hunt, and he had made a kill. Chiri increased his pace to a staghound's distance-eating run.

Three hundred yards away he came upon Link, a rifle in his right hand and a buck across his shoulders. Chiri spread his jaws in a canine grin, and his long body rippled as he galloped gracefully up to his master. Link grinned down at him.

"Hi. Hi, old dog. Bet you just came home 'cause you got hungry. Well, we can eat right hearty now. But Lud's been tied up since early morning, and you know how he hates to be alone. Let's move."

Side by side they came to the cabin, and the

lonesome Lud emerged from his kennel to whine a happy greeting. Link hung the buck in a tree, skinned it, and cut it up. He sliced two steaks from a haunch and thoughtfully regarded what remained. A trapper always gambled with fate. Sometimes he made a rich haul, and other years he didn't earn enough money to pay expenses. This had been such a year. Never had he worked harder, but there were scarcely enough furs in his cache to pay for the supplies he'd need next season. Still, with Chiri's help, he'd stuck it out. The wilderness had not whipped him and he was glad. Next year would bring another trapping season.

Link gave a fresh steak to Lud and one to Chiri. Then he re-entered the cabin, took a seasoned haunch of venison from his cold cellar, sliced a steak for himself, and built a fire. He heated a skillet and laid the steak in it. Making a wry face, he sat down to eat. Months had elapsed since he had had any-thing except meat. He would, he decided, trade all the venison or moose steaks north of the Gander for a can of tomatoes or a single cup of flour.

Outside, Chiri and Lud suddenly started an up-roar. Link pushed his plate back, leaped to his feet, and snatched at his rifle. There had been no human visitors on the Gander since last summer and it was unlikely that any were coming now. A moose, deer, or bear must be prowling around the cabin. Even though the game was coming back, hunting was none too good; it was best not to miss any chances. Link swung the door open and stared in amazement at the three horses fording the Gander.

Two carried packs; water lapped at the bottoms of the tarpaulins that covered them. The third horse bore a rider who sagged wanly forward, clutching at the saddle horn with his right hand. His left arm, bound with sapling branches, hung straight and stiff at his side. With mounting surprise Link recognized Constable John Murdock, from Masland. The dripping horses climbed out of the river and stood with their ears cocked forward, looking curiously at Link.

"Hi, John. What's the trouble?" Link called.

"Broken arm. I was coming into Two Bird Cabin when a grizzly spooked my horse. He pitched me off."

"Let me help you."

"I'll manage."

But despite that stout assertion, John Murdock half fell from his horse into Link Stevens' arms. Link passed the officer's right arm about his neck, and supported the other's shoulders as he helped him to a chair in the cabin. Two Bird Cabin was a long day's ride from the Gander. It was almost incredible that a man should be able to set his own broken arm, however crudely, pack horses, saddle another, and still ride on to the Gander. But John Murdock had done it.

"We'll have you fixed up in a jiffy," Link said

cheerfully. He split long splints from a block of wood and shaved them down with his knife. "When'd you get into Two Bird?"

"Night before last. Laid over one day."

"Sissy!" Link jibed. "Stay off the trail just because you've got a broken arm!"

John Murdock grinned feebly. "Yeah. How'd you do on the trap-lines this winter, Link?"

"I didn't make my beans and I've been eating nothing except meat for the past hundred years. I'll be glad to take you into Masland and see some civilization for a change."

"I reckon it would go good."

"It'll go fine." Link cut off the crude splints on John Murdock's arm and used the point of his knife to split the jacket and shirt sleeve. The constable's arm was discolored and swollen, but it seemed like a clean break. Link said quietly, "This is going to hurt, John."

"Yeah. I reckon."

Great beads of sweat stood out on the constable's forehead as Link straightened the arm. Murdock bit his lower lip; a gasp of pain escaped him. Link worked as swiftly as he could. Probing with his fingers, he felt the two ends of the broken bone grate together. He continued to pull and turn. Then, mercifully, John Murdock fainted. Link worked faster. The ends of the broken bone slipped into place and he bound them there. Then he splinted the arm. The constable groaned faintly and opened his eyes.

"Go ahead," he whispered.

"It's all done."

"Oh. Thanks, Link."

Supporting Murdock's shoulders, Link helped him over to the bunk, pulled off his boots, and covered him with blankets. The constable moaned and tossed for a moment, then fell into an exhausted sleep. Link stole quietly out to care for the horses.

He removed the saddle and bridle, and picketed the saddle horse with a long rope. Then he took the packs from the pack horses, hobbled them, and carried the packs into the cabin. Link unbound them, and drooled as he came upon a small parcel of dried peaches which the constable carried along. He slipped one into his mouth. Ordinarily he would have considered it a tasteless thing, dry and hard, but now it seemed the most delicious confection he had ever eaten.

John Murdock began to twist and mutter in his sleep. Link stole over to the bunk to quiet him, and as he did so he caught snatches of the injured man's disjointed conversation. "Yes, sir. The Caribou Range. I can get there. Yes, I understand."

Link laid a cool, wet cloth on Murdock's hot forehead. Remaining quietly beside the bunk, he watched his patient. The constable continued to twist and mutter. Then, shortly after midnight, his fever subsided and he slept quietly. Link crawled into the other bunk.

When he awakened, the early morning sun was shining through the cabin window. Link rose, slipped quietly over, and looked down at John Murdock. The constable was peacefully and comfortably asleep. Link stole quietly out of the cabin, to be greeted by Chiri.

He let his hand stray down to the big dog's ears, while Chiri pressed against him and wagged his tail. There was a rattling of Lud's chains as Lud came from his kennel and stretched. Link looked thoughtfully at the cabin door.

Since coming into Two Bird Cabin, John Murdock must have been through agony. To break an arm was bad enough. To be helpless and alone with a broken arm must be ten times as bad. Yet, in his feverish sleep, Murdock had still spoken of going to the Caribou Mountains—an unknown and forsaken range to the north. What was in the Caribous that must be investigated?

Link loosed Lud, and the dog galloped off, overcome with joy to be free of his chain after a long period of confinement. Chiri trotted with him. Link watched the two dogs, and tried to shrug his curiosity away. He was a trapper, and if he attended to all his own affairs which needed attention, he would have no time for anything else. Whatever lay in the Caribous wasn't his worry.

Link reached up to take a coiled fishing line from a nail beneath the snow shelter that overhung the cabin's door. Ordinarily, when he left the Gander, he did so before the spring breakup. This year, because he had taken such a poor catch of fur, he had stayed behind for the spring muskrat trapping. Now he awaited only a run-off of some of the flooded streams before going to Masland with such furs as he had. Meanwhile he must feed himself and his two dogs as best he could.

Chiri and Lud followed as he went down to the river and cut a stiff willow pole with his clasp knife. Link tied his fish line to it, kicked a rotten log apart, found some white grubs, baited, and cast. The hook sailed into the swift water and drifted downstream. Link retrieved and cast again, and again. On his fourth cast the line straightened and began to move directly across the river.

Link struck hard. The willow pole bent and the line tightened. Without undue ceremony, because he was fishing for food and not for sport, Link hauled a four-pound bull trout into the bank and scooped it up. He put the fish in a safe place, rebaited, and cast again. Ten minutes later he had a smaller trout.

Link untied the fishing line, coiled it, hung it over his shoulder, and picked up a trout in each hand. Returning to the cabin, he chained Lud and split the smaller trout. He gave half to Lud and half to Chiri. With two strokes of the axe he removed the head and tail from the larger fish, and divided those between the dogs. Slicing deep along the backbone, Link separated the fillets and carried them into the cabin.

John Murdock was still asleep, and Link moved softly as he poured water into a tin basin. He added salt, dropped the two boneless halves of the trout into it, and went down to the river for another pail of water. Carefully, rattling no lids and making no unnecessary noise, he built a fire and put a lump of bear grease into his big skillet. Measuring out four spoons of Murdock's coffee, he poured four cups of water on top of it and put the coffee pot on a hot lid. Link drooled as the spicy odor came up to tickle his nostrils. He had run out of coffee weeks ago.

John Murdock stirred in the bunk, then sat up to rub startled eyes.

"Hey! Why didn't you wake me?"

"What for? You couldn't have gone anywhere."

The injured man swung his legs over the side of the bunk. Link dropped the two halves of trout into the skillet and sprinkled them with salt. The constable wrinkled his nose.

"What's that? It smells good."

"Bull trout."

"Fresh?"

"It was swimming twenty minutes ago."

"Oh boy!" John Murdock moved suddenly,

winced, looked down at his splinted arm, and grinned. He rose, and on stocking feet padded over to the table. His nose wrinkled appreciatively.

"Haven't had any since last summer."

"You real fond of it, John?"

"I could eat trout three times a day."

Link said dryly, "I'll swap you my share for enough flour to make a mess of flapjacks."

"Good Lord! Take the flour anyway, man! If you look hard enough you'll even see a can of syrup."

"Syrup! The real honest-to-John article?" Link turned the two halves of trout in their sputtering grease and mixed a flapjack batter. He put the trout on a plate.

"Come and get it!"

As Murdock hungrily attacked the fish, Link spilled flapjacks onto a hot griddle, turned them, and slid them on a plate. Then he sat down, pouring a generous amount of syrup from the small tin Murdock had brought along. Almost ecstatically he began to eat. When his plate was empty, he pushed it aside, sighing contentedly.

"What do you know about the Caribou Mountains?" Murdock asked.

"I know they're a good place to stay out of. Hi Macklin's brother started for them three years ago, along with Tom Dosee. That's the last anybody ever heard or saw of them."

"Well, that's where I'm going."

"You're crazy!"

John Murdock shook his head. "Link, I have to go. Did you ever hear of Trigg Antray?"

Link wrinkled his forehead. "The name seems familiar."

"Probably it is. Antray's the naturalist-lecturer. It seems he got an idea there's albino moose in the Caribous, so he hired a bush pilot, man named Tom Garridge, to fly him in so he could find out. The plane conked out over the Caribous, but they got down safely. We know that because there was a radio message. Somebody's got to go to help 'em out, and I'm elected."

"You can't make it. That's a two-fisted country, and you've got only one."

Murdock shrugged. "This arm will knit as well on the trail as it will anywhere else if I take it easy. The way the rivers are, it'll take a long while to get back to Masland and send another man in my place. By that time Antray and Garridge may be dead."

"You'll be dead if you go. Haven't they sent any search planes in?"

"Half a dozen. They couldn't see a thing."

"Be reasonable, man! You can't get even near the Caribous with that broken arm! I've been forty or so miles northwest of the Gander, and that's tough country!"

"I still aim to try."

Link sat back, tilting his chair and looking hard at

John Murdock. Obviously the man meant what he said. He had been ordered to go into the Caribous to find two men who'd crashed there, and he meant to go even though he must know that he would probably sacrifice his own life if he did.

"You don't have to go," Link said quietly.

"Why not?"

"Because I'm going."

"You!"

"That's right. If anybody can get through and find your men, Chiri and I can do it."

"But—"

"Let's call it settled," Link said. "You've got two choices. Either I take you back to Masland, or you let Chiri and me go on while you stay here and rest up. As soon as you're able, ride back to Masland and tell 'em what happened. I'd like to have you bring a load of grub here, though. When I come back I'll need it."

"I can't do that!"

"You're going to do it. Somebody has to search the Caribous. Right? You can't do it and I can. That's all there is to it."

"Do you know the country?"

"As well as anyone does; there are no reliable maps. I don't see how I can miss the Caribous. They seem to stick far enough into the sky."

"Take my horses, then," Murdock said, weakening.

"No thanks. I'll travel light and fast with Chiri."

"Link, I'll never forget this! I'll make it up to you somehow! I'll—!"

"Aw, shut up or I'll break your other arm!"

Link rose and took his rifle from its peg. Chiri sprang to his feet expectantly. The big dog loved to hunt with Link, even though he had not yet achieved an understanding of the fine partnership that can exist between a man and his hunting dog. Having always hunted for himself, Chiri could see no reason why he should do otherwise, or why everything else was not capable of getting its own game. The idea of trailing game for Link had never occurred to him.

"There's most of a deer in the cellar," Link told Murdock, "but I'd better be sure you have plenty of grub. You may be here a while."

"I have supplies. You can help yourself to 'em."

"If you twisted my arm, I might steal that parcel of dried peaches."

"You'll steal more than that. I appreciate this, Link. I know I wouldn't have one chance in fifty of getting through, but somebody has to go. I—"

"You carry on like a gabby old squirrel," Link said. "I've always wanted a good excuse to go into the Caribous. So kindly keep your big trap shut."

Once outside he was deadly serious. The Caribous were a forbidden range, an unknown stretch of peaks lying deep within one of the last great virgin wildernesses. As far as he knew no man had ever entered them—and come out again. His plans had to be made carefully.

Chiri ranged into the spruces to do some hunting of his own. Link stayed on the trail, solemnity tempered by an elation which he could not suppress. What would he find in the Caribous? At any rate, he had committed himself to going, and now there was no turning back. Link grinned wryly, knowing that he didn't want to turn back.

At a motion in the spruces, Link halted. He saw a young deer, sleek and trim in its spring coat, racing toward him. Thirty paces behind it, gaining fast on the small buck, came Chiri.

Link raised his rifle, sighted, and awaited the right moment. When the running deer entered a thinner growth of spruces he shot, and the little buck dropped in its tracks. Chiri came up, wagging his tail and panting slightly as he looked at the kill. He could have brought it down, but they had game, and he knew Link would share it with him. Link dressed the small deer and gave Chiri a generous slice of the liver. Then he shouldered the deer, carried it back to camp, and hung it in a tree. Lud came out of his kennel, sitting expectantly by and knowing that he, too, would feed soon. Murdock appeared at the cabin door.

"I'll carry some along but leave most for you," Link said. "You may need it."

"Doubt if I can handle a rifle," the constable said ruefully.

"No need to now, and you can always use your belt gun if you have to shoot. Anyhow, there's lots of fishing tackle here; you'll be able to catch trout in a few days."

Link skinned and quartered the deer. Laying the quarters on the fresh skin, he cut the large bones out of them. He threw one to Lud, who fell upon it and started chewing happily. Chiri, already fed, disdained any more. Link arranged the boneless quarters in a neat pile. The only means of transportation he had was his own back and Chiri's. Every ounce counted, and it would be wasting energy to carry bones. Link left a piece of the meat where Chiri could find it, as he did not want the big dog to go hunting tonight, and hung the rest in the dug-out cellar beneath his cabin. In this country the ground never thawed beneath topsoil depth. It was easy to make a natural and permanent refrigerator merely by digging.

He climbed back into the cabin and began arranging the articles he would need. The Caribous were strictly an unknown quantity; he had no way of knowing how long it would take to reach and climb into them, or what he might need. Link laid out needles and thread, a few first-aid articles, knives, his sleeping bag, a skillet and pot, and his rifle. He laid an axe and a hundred feet of rope beside the articles he had arranged, then looked dubiously at his rifle. The day the black wolf's pack had attacked him, he had broken the rifle's firing pin and later replaced it with a laboriously filed nail. Nails, however, were soft metal. There was no telling when this one would wear out, and there weren't any stores in the Caribous.

"Something wrong with your rifle, Link?" Murdock asked.

"Broken firing pin."

"Take mine. I have a hundred and twenty cartridges for it. You can have the revolver, too, if you need it."

"Thanks, John. The rifle will be enough."

Link added fishing line and hooks to his collection. He wrapped one of the boneless hind-quarters of venison in a discarded flour sack and stood back to inspect the load. Chiri could pack about forty-five pounds, while Link himself could take a little more. As though reading his thoughts, John Murdock spoke.

"Fill it up, Link. That's the very least you can do."

"Fill what up?"

"Your grub list. There's plenty here."

"You might need that yourself."

"Don't be foolish. I left Masland equipped for the Caribous. There'll be plenty for me if all I'm going to do is hang around here a while and go back to Masland."

"Well . . ."

"Pack it, or I'll do it myself!"

Link poured flour into three canvas containers, and took a portion of coffee, sugar, tea, rice, dried beans, dried peas, and baking powder. Murdock pressed the parcel of dried peaches and the can of syrup upon him, then looked at the pile of supplies thoughtfully.

"You still haven't got very much. You could pack another forty pounds if you used both your dogs."

Link shook his head. "Chiri can rustle his own grub if necessary. Lud can't. I'll leave him here to keep you company."

The sun had not yet risen the next morning when Link called Chiri to the cabin door. He strapped the dog's pack on, then shouldered his own. Link turned to the constable.

"So long, John. Be seeing you!"

2

Barrier

Three days later, a roughly estimated fifty miles from the Gander, Link came to a north-flowing river that foamed whitely between high cut banks. He stood beside it, the pack-laden Chiri poising expectantly with him, and watched a big bull moose with velvet-covered bumps of antlers walk along the other side. Link re-checked the compass course he had set for himself.

If he had calculated correctly, and travelled in the right direction, the Caribous would lie somewhere in the dense wilderness still ahead of him. Now, however, he had to swerve and cross this river. Link studied it with the eye of an experienced river man.

It was very swift; evidently it pitched down a steep decline here. Angry white water snarled against both banks, and the center was an unbroken current. The river could not be crossed at this point. Nor was there any indication, any gentle riffles or quiet pools, that it became quieter down-stream. Link marked a white birch that leaned over the opposite bank. It was a peculiarly shaped tree, slanting over the water; its lower branches had been carried away by chunks of ice that had bumped against them. Link fixed in his mind the general contours of the terrain around the tree, and remem-bered that fresh moose tracks should pass just to the left of it. When he was certain that he would know the tree when he came to it, and could pick up his compass course there, he started upstream.

A fluttering excitement grew within him. This river, which joined the Gander far to the north, was called the Goose, but other than that it was almost unknown. At various times Link had talked with Indians and trappers who knew part of it, but the country beyond was almost untrod by human feet. Certainly the only trails would be game paths. The best he could do was keep on the course he had set and get through in any way he could.

The river had to have a fording place, and an hour after he swerved Link's ears told him that he was approaching it. He heard a murmur, like a far-off wind, and twenty minutes later came to a falls that pitched over a thirty-foot rock ledge. Link looked at the wide sheet of falling water. Spray rose from the foot and drifted like miniature clouds out over the spruces.

Extending a hundred feet downstream from the

foot of the falls was a comparatively quiet pool, where the force of the falling water had hollowed a bed in the river's bottom. Link looked critically at the pool. It was deep and about forty yards wide. Where the pool ended was snarling white water, through which no craft could live or be guided once it was in that foaming spray. But Link thought the pool could be crossed if he stayed out of the white water.

Across the river a timber wolf began to moan. Another joined it, then two more. Chiri pricked up his ears and looked toward the sound, knowing that the wolves had a den across the river and that two of those moaning were cubs of the year before. They would stay with their parents until fall, then seek dens of their own. The dog glanced indifferently away; he was not afraid of wolves.

Link stripped Chiri's pack off and hung it in a tree. Work made the big dog hungry, and if he was given the opportunity, he might eat some or all of the food in his pack. Free, Chiri walked unhesitatingly down to the river and plunged into the ice-cold water. He swam halfway across, then turned to come smoothly back. Link watched carefully, for this was one means of gauging the current's strength. Chiri hadn't been troubled by swift water.

Link took an axe from his pack and set to work felling a dead pine. Chiri wandered into the forest. He was willing to work whenever Link wished him to, but he understood that stripping his pack, or freeing him from harness, was granting him freedom. Nervous and energetic, he always wanted to know what lay about him.

Link mopped his brow and stood back. The tree upon which he worked had been long dead, but was by no means rotten. Its trunk was tough and solid throughout. Link took a whetstone from his pocket and honed a fresh edge on the axe. He tested the blade on his arm, and when it was sharp enough to shave hairs off he resumed chopping. The dead tree fell amid a shower of splintering branches and cracking twigs. Link cut the larger branches off, then fashioned a wooden wedge and sank his axe lengthwise into the trunk. Making a slit, he forced the wedge in and pounded it home with the flat of his axe. The trunk started to split. Link hammered more wedges in until the trunk lay in two clean halves. He chopped them into even lengths and carried them down to the pool.

On the other side of the river, the denned timber wolves moaned warningly. Chiri emerged from the forest and moved down beside Link.

Removing his trail boots and socks, Link entered the water and shivered as its icy sting crept up his legs. He floated two of the split logs and bound them tightly with his rope. He added another, and another, until he had a sizeable raft. Then he crossed the rope and bound the other end. Holding the rope's end in his hand, he tied it to a rock on the bank while the raft floated free.

He stood back to inspect his work, muttering because he had forgotten to bring a handful of spikes. They were much better than rope as well as faster, and when the wilderness traveller wished to leave his raft he had only to pull the spikes out until he came to the next river. However, rope would have to do. Link tested the raft, which sank only slightly under his weight. He stepped ashore, cut a long pushing pole, and laid it on the bank.

It was too late to cross the river tonight and he might as well camp here. Link spread his sleeping bag. He gathered twigs for kindling and larger pieces of wood to keep a night fire. He dug a coil of fishing line out of his pack, strung it to a cut pole, baited the hook with a chunk of moose meat, and cast into the pool. Almost before it hit the water, something seized the bait. Link struck hard, and a broad grin overspread his face. This was new and good country, almost untouched. Whatever had hit his bait was bigger, and fought harder, than any fish he could remember. It was a stiff fight to play it in even with a stout willow pole. Link whistled when he saw the trout. It was a bull trout, or Dolly Varden, but there were few fish like it on the Gander. Link reached down to pass his fingers through its gills, and flung the fish up on the bank. It was more than big enough to provide supper and breakfast for himself and Chiri. Link built a cooking fire, cooked the fish, and ate. But Chiri had wandered away and was still coursing out in the brush.

Furtive rustlings told of other animals that moved about in the brush. Link lay back, pillowing his head in cupped hands, completely satisfied. The night overflowed with sound and hints of sound, and he interpreted everything as he heard it. Trappers, he decided, were fools as well as gamblers. He had spent a fruitless winter on the Gander when, if he had moved only fifty miles to the northwest, he would have been in the midst of plenty. That was something to remember. The game did not disappear, it merely moved. If only a man would look for it, instead of waiting for fortune to come to him, he could not go unrewarded.

There was a moving shadow outside the circle of light cast by the fire. Chiri came in to lay his head on Link's knee. Having already fed on game which he himself had pulled down, the big dog scorned the fish Link offered him and curled up to sleep. A chill stole into the night. Link sought his sleeping bag, and for a while lay staring at the millions of bright stars that glowed overhead. The next time he looked the stars had paled and it was early morning.

Link rose, re-kindled his fire, and heated some of the fish he had cooked the night before. When Chiri came expectantly up, Link fed him a tiny bit. Ordinarily working dogs should eat only at the end of each working day; to feed them sooner meant that they were apt to become listless on the trail. Besides, Chiri would never go with too little food. If he did not get as much as he thought Link should give him, he would always catch his own.

Link inspected his raft which, after floating all night, still rode high and dry in the water. Carefully he looked at the packs. With a long hank of fish line, he tied a piece of dry pine to everything that might sink if it went into the water. Floating to the top, the wood would act as a marker buoy and enable him to recover whatever might accidentally be swept overboard. Anything that floated would never be recovered in the swift current. Link mounted his raft.

"Chiri!" he called.

The big dog came down and put an experimental paw on the raft. Then, as Link grabbed at him, he leaped back. Chiri was not afraid of water which he tackled under his own power. But having never ridden on a man-made craft of any description, he hadn't the slightest intention of trying one now.

"Come here, you old fool!" Link said angrily.

Chiri retreated up the bank, wagging his tail and looking quizzically at Link. Link muttered under his breath, glowering at the dog. Catching up the pushing pole, he cast the rope off and started across the pool; let the fool swim if he wouldn't ride! As soon as he started, Chiri jumped in and started to swim. He paddled around and around the raft, obviously enjoying himself.

Link re-set his pole, keeping the raft straight in the swift water and leaving a purling wake behind as he set a course for the opposite bank. He had judged the current with his eyes, had watched Chiri swim into it, and had decided that he could cross safely. Link relaxed. Though swift, the water was not fierce. Link set his pole again, deeply, then flung himself down to avoid being yanked from the raft. Behind him, thrust deeply into mud, the pole remained imbedded in the pool. The raft started toward the foaming snarl downstream.

Hurriedly Link began to unlace his boots, preparatory to leaping in and towing the raft. The makeshift craft, caught in a stronger current, swung downstream faster. Chiri circled closer, curious as to what his master was doing. Desperately Link flung himself full length, extended his stretched arm as far as it would go, and grasped Chiri's soaked tail. The startled dog struck powerfully for the opposite stream bank; the raft floated smoothly behind him.

As soon as it grounded in the shallows Link leaped off. Keeping hold of the end of rope, he towed the raft in to the bank and secured it. Chiri shook himself and wagged up to Link, who grinned as he scratched the big dog's ears.

"Thanks," he said. "You were just in time."

Link carried the packs ashore and took the raft apart. Two by two he dragged the logs far enough up on the bank so that no flood water could sweep them away. Probably he would want to return by this route. Finding the logs waiting for him would save the necessity of cutting more. Then, packing Chiri, Link shouldered his own pack and walked downstream to the tree he had marked yesterday.

Day after day, fighting his way through or around sucking and treacherous muskeg, cutting a path where impassable alder thickets opposed him, wading the rivers he could wade and rafting across those he could not, he travelled along the compass course he had set for himself. From the first he had carefully rationed the supplies brought from the Gander and taken much of his living from the country he moved through, and here it was easier to do that. The Gander had been a land of starvation, but there was a lavish abundance west of the Goose. Deer snorted at him, then stole quietly into their secret thickets. Moose pounded through the brush. Squirrels chattered in every tree. Black bears prodded for grubs or dug for ground squirrels. All the rivers were filled with fish. He could almost have his choice of wild food, and even though he worked hard every day, Chiri grew fat. At the same time Link trod cautiously and always with his rifle ready.

This was grizzly country and, like all who know

them, Link had a great respect for the ponderous bears. Grizzlies might decide to do anything on the spur of the moment, and they were always clever as well as hard to stop. At least twice a day, and once three times in a single hour, Link halted and stopped Chiri while a grizzly lolling in the path he wished to follow made up its mind to get out of the way.

As he travelled, so gradually that the change was almost imperceptible, the character of the country underwent an almost complete transformation. Instead of sluggish flat-country water, the streams and rivers were swift, thus all mountain-fed. There was little muskeg and the trees were larger, though fewer. The forest had more pine and fir with not as much spruce.

One afternoon Link broke over the top of a forested knoll into the edge of a clearing. At the far side, a medium-sized grizzly was busy digging. Link stopped to watch, interested in the bear's actions. The grizzly scraped with both front paws, sending a spray of brown dirt between his rear legs. His head and front quarters disappeared as he enlarged the hole.

Suddenly and without any warning whatever he flung out of the excavation and at top speed hurtled across the clearing straight at Link. His head was raised, mouth open; his hackles bristled. Chiri darted into the clearing where he would have more room to dodge and whirl if a fight came. Link raised his rifle and sighted.

He squeezed the trigger. As though it had been flicked by an invisible lance, the hair on the bear's chest parted and fell back into place. Link shot again, trying hard to keep cool and aim well. He ejected the empty shell and shot a third time. The grizzly stumbled, and stopped. For a moment he stood still. A final roar escaped him as he tried to renew his charge. He could not. The grizzly staggered, walked in a crazy little half circle, and went down.

Regretfully Link walked up to the fallen beast. The grizzly had offered him no alternative. If Link had not killed him, certainly he would have done his best to kill Link. Probably, Link decided, the grizzly had seen him the moment he broke over the knoll, but had continued to dig in an effort to deceive him into thinking himself unseen. When Link came no nearer, the bear launched his charge anyway.

Link looked sharply, attracted by an unusual hump under the grizzly's fur. He knelt, and reached down to feel the hard end of a bit of wood. Link cut the fur away, and examined with mounting astonishment the broken end of what had evidently been an arrow. Probing carefully with his knife, Link removed the six inches of shaft that was imbedded in the bear's flank, and his astonishment increased.

The arrow's shaft had been crudely fashioned from a yellow-birch wand, but the point was a roughly hammered, empty jacket for a 30-06 cartridge! Link turned it over and over in his hand, while all the terrible implications of this wild drama unfolded themselves. Three years ago, when Hi Macklin's brother had left Masland with the avowed intention of seeing whatever lay in the Caribous, he had packed a 30-06. He must have lost that rifle, or spent all the cartridges he carried, to have been desperate enough to tackle a grizzly with a crudely made arrow. Link shuddered. Tom Macklin's bones probably lay somewhere in the shadow cast by the forbidding Caribous.

Miles to the northwest, so far away that it somehow seemed unreal, a patch of white thrust into the sky. It might have been a white cloud, except that the sky was cloudless. Link stared in fascination; it was a cloud-covered peak of the almost mythical Caribous. He looked away and back again, as though the peak actually were something born in his imagination and would disappear any second. It was still there, still supporting the weight of snow that it held toward the sky. A cold shiver rippled up his spine. Hi Macklin's brother must have had the same view!

That night Link made his camp on the site of a sloping ridge, near a spring that bubbled out. To conserve his supplies, he set rabbit snares. He might have brought some of the grizzly, but bear meat, and especially grizzly, was apt to be stringy and tasteless stuff. He would eat it only when nothing better offered.

Link gathered firewood, for this high country was much colder, and then made the rounds of his rabbit snares. He took three big snowshoe hares out of five snares and gathered the other two unsprung. Chiri went away to do his own hunting, but was back in less than an hour. Obviously there was plenty of game.

With early dawn Link went on. At high noon he mounted a sparsely forested ridge and looked again at the snow peaks in the distance. They were clearer now, with their rugged outlines much more sharply defined. A belt of forest strapped their lower reaches, and encircled them more than halfway to the top. Beyond, as nearly as Link could see, were bare meadows and beyond the meadows glaciers which clung precariously to the cliffs or filled the gullies. Patches of windswept rock thrust gaunt heads out of the snow. Twin spires rose over what seemed to be a pass, and Link marked it carefully. He would set his course straight toward the spires.

Chiri pricked up his ears and looked down the slope. Link followed his gaze. There was a small creek tumbling down a valley, into an open meadow. As Link watched, two lumbering grizzlies emerged from the forest and prodded about the meadow. Finally, unhurriedly, they ambled up the creek's winding course. Link walked down the slope, and almost stumbled into three bull moose that were resting on the sheltered side of a knoll. The bulls loped awkwardly away, their sleek muscles rippling as they moved, but a herd of buck deer that passed to the windward side merely stopped to stare.

Link pondered, trying to account for the actions of these animals. Bull moose wouldn't always run even back on the Gander, but deer invariably fled. This country was far wilder than the Gander and less hunted; less timidity was to be expected in the animals. Then the wind changed. Hoisting white tails over their backs, the deer bobbed gracefully away. Link pursed his lips thoughtfully.

Deer lacked unusually keen vision, but he had been near enough so that this herd could tell him for what he was. Almost all animals depended upon a combination of sight, hearing, and scent, to advise them of danger. Why should bull moose flee at once, while smaller deer stood curiously until they got his scent? Another cold chill trembled down Link's spine as he found the answer.

This was almost virgin country! So few men had ever trod here that the deer had not even recognized him as a danger. It had been Chiri they had run from! They had caught the dog's odor, and that was enough like wolf scent to frighten them. But this wilderness was so deep and so isolated that animals had never seen and therefore were unafraid of man!

They had simply never been hunted, and game trails pounded throughout the centuries by herds of game were beaten deep into the earth. The country was crossed and re-crossed by hundreds of paths which, had they been found near a civilized community, would have been excellent bridle paths. Link followed one that led in the direction he wanted to travel, moving swiftly along on this unexpectedly easy route. He was almost completely out of the muskeg now, and there were few thickets.

But the country was heavily wooded. Link camped in forests so dense that, even when the sun was highest, light never reached the needle-littered ground. His fire cast a circle of light against the mighty tree trunks surrounding him. Once there was a startled 'whoof' as a grizzly coming down the slope smelled smoke and fled. Link hastily threw another armful of wood on his fire.

He slept only sporadically. Awakening at intervals, he saw Chiri sitting tensely in the outer circle of light. Link had always held the theory that a keen-nosed wild creature used its nose both to identify other creatures and to determine their intentions. He had seen feeding caribou stand placidly while well-fed wolves literally sniffed at their heels, while the same herd would flee in panic as soon as a hunting wolf came within scenting distance. Link did not understand how they knew whether the wolf was hunting, but they did. Now Link deduced from Chiri's actions that, though nothing dared come in to the fire, there were many things in the black forest whose curiosity had been aroused by these strange intruders in their domain.

With dawn, keeping Chiri close beside him, Link went on. The forest was so dense that he could see almost nothing. He must depend on Chiri to warn him of possible danger. However, though the big dog bristled a couple of times, nothing appeared.

Then the trees began to thin out and to grow smaller. They were climbing steadily, and the wind that blew from the snow banks and glaciers had an icy bite. Link buttoned his jacket a little more tightly and went on. Finally he broke out of the trees and was above timber line. Link stopped in his tracks.

A ram with a curling spread of horns stood less than forty feet away, watching him intently. Beyond were more sheep, dozens of smaller rams, ewes, and a few early born lambs. None except the big ram paid the slightest attention to him, and Link stared in disbelief. Mountain sheep were wild things, wary and keen-sighted. The most expert hunters considered themselves fortunate when they were able to stalk one successfully. It was incredible that an entire herd would let a man walk almost into their midst. There could be only one answer. If these sheep had ever seen any men, certainly they had not seen enough of them to be aware of any special danger.

Link shot a small ram. The animal dropped heavily, and a ewe standing near stared curiously at it. Link shook a wondering head. Even the blast of a rifle made no impression on these sheep. Hunting them was slaughter rather than sport, but he needed meat. And he had better cook it right here.

Above lay the snow fields, and there was no telling how long it would take to cross them. Certainly he would find no firewood in the snow; no trees grew so far up. Link dressed the small ram, built a fire, and spitted the sheep's quarters over it. Fat dribbled down; the fire sputtered and flared wherever it struck. Link turned the spitted quarters of the ram slowly, so that they would cook on all sides. He would have to camp here tonight; so much meat would take a long while to cook.

With morning he divided the roast mutton between his pack and Chiri's and made his way upward. Looking up from a long distance away, the peaks had not seemed unusually high. Now, looking down, he saw that he had climbed a tremendous distance. Foothills stretched away to the east, and beyond them were the spruces and muskeg through which he had fought his way. But the twin spires still towered a long way over him. What lay beyond them?

They came to a solid rock cliff that swept far above them and effectively blocked the path. Scrambling, sometimes on his hands and knees, Link fought his way up the gravelled slope to the left. He met another rock wall, and worked his way along a ledge until the ledge ended and he stared down into dizzying space. There was nothing to do except go back and try another route.

Link returned the way he had come, and camped that night at the foot of the wall where he had swerved. This was absolutely barren country, with only gnarled shrubs and sparse grass growing between snow banks. There was no possibility of keeping a fire. Link glanced wistfully toward the forest he had left. But going back down and returning would consume valuable time, and he wanted an early start. Besides, though he probably would spend a cold night here, it should not be a dangerous one. It was not likely that any animals would climb this far. They would stay down where they did their hunting.

Link unpacked and fed Chiri, ate some mutton, and crawled into the sleeping bag. Light snow was falling. Warm in his sleeping bag, Link dozed. He did not know what time he was awakened by Chiri's furious snarl.

He sat up, reaching for his rifle. The snow had stopped, and in the dim light scattered by the stars he saw Chiri a few feet away. The big dog faced into the darkness, snarling continuously. A pebble rattled down the opposite slope, then its noise was suddenly muffled as it stopped abruptly in the snow. Link tried to see what had dislodged the pebble, but could not. Crawling out of his sleeping bag, he stood there with the rifle ready. From far up the side of the cliff, another pebble rattled down. Link remained out in the open; he had guessed wrong when he decided that nothing would come here.

Chiri's snarls bubbled away to nothingness.

When daylight finally came, Link saw the track of a grizzly in the snow, less than twenty feet from where he had slept. He shivered. Had the grizzly decided to attack he could not have stopped it. But it had gone on, obviously intending to cross into the Caribous. In so doing it had shown him a path.

Link followed the grizzly's track up the slope, then onto a ledge on the face of the cliff. Chiri, with nothing except space to receive him should he make a misstep, trotted unconcernedly ahead.

In the middle of the day they came out on top of the mountain, between the stone spires. Deep snow lay here; the tracks of the grizzly were plain in it, and had broken a path. Link followed as swiftly as he could, hoping to get into timber, or at least to firewood, before night.

But luck was against him. First a few black clouds scudded across the sky, then a high wind screamed across the mountain. Snow whirled down, then flew so thickly that Link could scarcely see the dog at his side.

He was aware that Chiri turned and faced away from him, looking toward a tangled pile of rocks. When Link stopped he advanced toward them. Link followed. He saw the black mouth of a cave gaping in the snow-whitened rocks, and walked cautiously to it. The mountain storm was so furious that he could not go on, and the cave would at least offer shelter. Link picked up a small rock and tossed it within the black opening. Nothing happened. He entered the cave and struck a match.

Its flickering light revealed a grinning human skull.

3
Cougar's Den

Link let the match burn almost down to his fingers, and in the half-light that filtered into the cave he continued for a moment to stare at the dimly seen skull. Some other traveller had found his way this far into the Caribous. Probably, like Link, he had been caught in the heights by a sudden storm and had taken refuge in the cave. He had never got out of it.

Outside the wind screamed harder, and snow whirled down so thickly that the mouth of the cave was almost hidden. The light inside equalled that of late evening, just before night closes completely down. In the darkness, Link groped with Chiri's pack, unfastened it, and cast his own down. He could not make a safe way in the blinding storm, and regardless of the fate of the other wayfarer, he would stay.

Chiri paced to the mouth of the cave and lay down, while blowing snow powdered his face and forequarters. Link spread his sleeping bag and, feeling his way, he cut a generous slice of mutton for himself and one for Chiri. The big dog came to get his food, but carried it back to the mouth of the cave before he ate. It was from that direction that possible danger would come, and Chiri wanted to be ready for it.

Link walked to the mouth of the cave, crowded in beside Chiri, and tried to look out. The wind still screamed across the heights, and snow fell fast. Link began to think about the other man who had sought shelter in the cave. Maybe he had become snowbound there, and unable to get out of the heights. It was quite possible. He himself would have to wait out the storm and see what conditions were like after it was over.

He walked back to his pack and rummaged in it until his fingers closed about one of the three candles he had brought along. He lit it, shielding the flame with his hand. When the wick had a good light he held it aloft. The flame bent inward, toward the back of the cave, but it did not blow out. Link gasped.

The back of the cave was literally carpeted with the bones of animals—and the unmistakable remains of a man! Shreds of clothing were mixed with the bones. The paw prints of a great cat were very much in evidence in the soft earth on the cave's floor. This was not a casual cave, but a cougar's den!

Link looked back at Chiri, still guarding the entrance, then knelt beside the human skeleton. This man was no storm-pressed wayfarer who had sought temporary shelter in the cave. He had been killed outside and dragged in here. The polished bones had been cracked by powerful jaws. Link picked up a bit of cloth and held the candle very near so he could see it. It was wool, the sort of clothing hunters and trappers wore, but otherwise it told him nothing. Maybe Tom Dosee or Hi Macklin's brother had ended his journey here. Certainly the skeleton had been there far too long to be that of either of the men he was searching for.

Gently Link laid the bit of cloth back, and held the candle high enough so he could look at the rest of the litter in the cave. Doubtless, like Link, the stranger had stumbled onto one of the few places, possibly the only one, where the Caribous could be crossed. This crossing was also used by herds of sheep and goats that wanted to get from one slope to the other. The cougar had only to lie in wait until something he wanted came along. Link looked once more at all that remained of the other wayfarer.

There were cougars back on the Gander, but they were timid, self-effacing creatures which never showed themselves to man if they could possibly avoid it. No man ever saw one unless it was trapped or treed by dogs. But this cougar, high on the Caribous' rocky slopes, made no distinction between man and beast. In fact, in this country no beast, even normally timid ones, seemed to be afraid of man. Link pondered the significance of that.

For all practical purposes, then, these strictly wild animals still lived a Stone Age existence. From the beginning of time their basic law, the law of survival, had not changed. The Caribous were actually so little known and so little visited that, when he came there, man was just another Stone Age creature, too. It seemed incredible. If true, it meant that when Link got down the other side of the mountain—always supposing that he did get there—he would be able to hold his own only if he was and remained stronger than whatever he met. There would be no fear of man to help him.

Link glanced at Chiri, still alert in the mouth of the cave, and felt reassured. Thanks to his early wilderness life, the dog was virtually a Stone Age beast himself, and probably more capable than Link of coping with whatever natural dangers they might find here. As far as Chiri was concerned, this world was no different from the one in which he had always lived. Chiri understood thoroughly the fact that the cougar might come back, he knew it was hostile, and he wished to be ready should it come. Link relaxed slightly. A man could go anywhere with Chiri, and his chances of getting there and coming back were about twice what they were without the big dog.

Link crawled into his sleeping bag, laid the rifle where he could seize it instantly, and prepared to sleep. Danger was present here, and fear, but so was companionship.

He slept lightly, his subconscious mind attuned to everything that took place. This was a woodsman's trick he had practised before. Before he went to sleep he had inspected the cave thoroughly and everything about it was firmly fixed in his mind. He would know should any changes occur. When Chiri shifted position he sat up, and again when the screaming wind died. Both times he saw the dog still in the cave's entrance, still watching. Link went back to sleep. The next time he awakened morning had come.

The wind had died last night and with it the snow must have stopped. Link walked to the mouth of the cave and looked out. Snow was no longer falling, but in sheltered spots it had been whipped into high drifts by the wind. Other places, high crags and smooth rock where the wind had had a clean sweep, were bare. Link ate more mutton, then strapped Chiri's pack on, shouldered his own, and stepped outside.

The wind had not died, he saw; it had merely stopped last night's wild screaming. Blowing over the snow fields, it had all the sting of deep and cold winter. Link felt slightly deaf. He did not know how high the Caribous were, but only very high altitudes could have so affected his ears.

The twin spires towered above him, and as Link watched, a patch of clinging snow near the top of one loosed its hold. It plunged down the precipice, starting more snow as it rolled, until finally the mountain itself seemed to be moving. Link walked back toward the mouth of the cave as tons of snow piled up at the foot of the spire. A white spume like that blown from the foot of a falls drifted away from it.

Link sighed as the magnitude of his task made itself apparent. On any map the Caribous were a mere pinprick, but once penetrated they were a huge wilderness. From where he stood Link saw other snow-clad peaks, some even taller than the one upon which he stood. He tried to form a plan of action.

Since he knew nothing about the Caribous, he would have to let circumstances dictate the future. He would have to do one thing at a time, and obviously the first step was to get off this peak.

The pack-laden Chiri plowed a little way through the snow and stopped in a tall drift that heaped itself over his shoulders. Link started out cautiously. Some of the snow in the heights must lay there all year. It could be very dangerous. During warm spells rivers of melted snow must flow from this peak; they would form crevices. More snow might bridge those crevices, and anything that fell through would stand little chance of getting out again.

Link mounted a wind-bared rock and looked about for animal tracks. There must be some safe route out of the heights and into the sheltered valleys below, and the animals would know where it was. However, no fresh tracks broke the new snow; evidently last night's storm had kept all animals out of the mountains. With Chiri pacing beside him, Link started down the slope. He dared not stay here. There was sufficient food remaining in the packs so that they could weather a short siege in the cougar's den, but if enough snow fell it might be weeks before they got out. Escape from the heights had to be risked now. If necessary, he could camp tonight in a snowbank.

Link threw himself suddenly backward, throwing his hands over his head and clawing at the snow behind him. Agile as a cat, Chiri leaped to one side. There had seemed to be only unbroken snow ahead, but when he stepped into it the snow started to roll. Evidently he had started across a weak snow bridge over an unseen crevice. Another cloud of snow and ice particles drifted into the air. Link held perfectly still, feeling himself begin to slip. Twenty feet away, safe, Chiri whined uneasily.

Very slowly, wriggling a hair's breadth at a time,

Link sought some solid thing against which he could rest his feet. He had held grimly on to the rifle. Now, an inch at a time, he elevated that so the muzzle pointed skyward. Suddenly he snapped the stock down into the snow. It held. Helping himself with the moored rifle, Link worked cautiously backward. Ten minutes after he fell, he stood once more on his feet, a safe distance from the end of the collapsed snow bridge.

Link retraced his steps cautiously. The snow was deceptive; it could cover sheer ice, mountain rocks, or nothing at all. He would have to watch his step much more carefully.

Chiri licked snow as he travelled. Watching him, Link realized how thirsty he was himself. He reached down to grab a double fistful. Packing it into a hard ball, he sucked it and let water run down his dry throat. Coming to another stretch of wind-bared rock, he stopped to look ahead. Even though there were both patches of bare rock and stretches of shallow snow between them, there were many areas of deep, soft snow. Plowing through them without snowshoes was hard, slow work.

Link unstrapped Chiri's pack and let the dog stretch. He unshouldered his own pack, and dug into it for the parcel of dried peaches which he had brought from the Gander. A sinking sensation entered the pit of his stomach as he realized how little civilized food remained. Link fed Chiri a piece of mutton and ate a dried peach. He ate another, then reluctantly replaced the parcel and rose, stamping his feet and beating his hands to warm himself. Re-packing Chiri, he continued through the snow fields, grumbling to himself as he walked. He should be coming to a slope, and timber, but evidently the top of this mountain ran on forever.

With a sudden little rush, Chiri was ahead of him. The big dog's ears were up, his tail wagged as he stared at a high snowbank. Link slipped his glove off and put his thumb on the hammer of his rifle. There was no telling what he might meet here, but he had better be prepared. Then Chiri bent his head to snuffle and Link saw the hole in the snowbank.

It was big and hard-packed, and a few silver hairs clung to the frozen bottom of the hole. Grizzly tracks led away from it, down the slope. Link nod-ded understandingly. The grizzly, too, must have decided to sleep through the storm instead of walk-ing it out. He had merely curled up and let the snow cover him, while heat from his own body melted the snow on which he lay. Link quickened his steps along the grizzly's trail. Since the big bear had known how to get up one side of the mountain, the chances were excellent that he also knew how to get down the other.

An hour before nightfall Link came to another cliff, a sheer rock wall that dropped three hundred feet to an above-timberline meadow. Snow lay in scattered patches on the wild upland pasture, and at the far side the green belt of forest began. But there was a ledge, as far as Link could see the only break on the cliff, and the grizzly had travelled it. Slowly, watching sharply for snow and the occasional patches of ice formed where water had seeped out of cracks in the rock, Link walked down the ledge. Chiri, as usual, walked unconcernedly beside or behind him.

An hour and a half later Link crouched over a crackling fire in the thin upper fringe of the forest. His kettle, filled with melted snow water, bubbled merrily and sent out the nose-tickling odor of hot coffee. Link fried mutton in his skillet, and ate a hot meal. Then he leaned contentedly back.

He was in the mythical Caribous at last. They were not the never-never country which story and legend had made them. They were a deep wilderness and very hard to reach, but they could be penetrated. He and Chiri had proved that.

There were furtive rustlings and shufflings both in the forest and about the meadow. A bear grunted. A deer called lonesomely. Sleepy birds twittered in the trees, and a white-footed mouse squeaked as it padded along a hidden highway. Link threw more wood on the fire and slept with his rifle in easy reach. Even in this wild country it was very unlikely that any beast would come in to a fire. However, Chiri would give him ample warning if it should happen.

Link awoke with early morning, re-kindled his fire, and cooked breakfast. He still had no definite plan and could form none until he knew more about the Caribous. He pursed thoughtful lips. It was necessary only to stand on top of the mountain he had crossed to know that the Caribous were a vast country. Hunting for any particular thing within them was a stupendous task. Supposing that Trigg Antray and Thomas Garridge actually had landed a plane in the mountains, it might be anywhere. However, had it landed in one of the upland meadows, it would have been seen by a search plane. Of course it might have crashed against a peak, started an avalanche, and been buried beneath tons of snow. In that event nobody would ever find it, or its passengers.

His mind made up, Link stamped his cooking fire into the earth and started out. He would first search the belts of forest and the sheltered valleys. A plane crashing in either place might be hidden from the air, though undoubtedly it would mow down enough trees and shrubs to be perfectly evident to anyone who came near it on foot.

Chiri suddenly growled. Link whirled, raising his rifle as he did so and snapping the hammer back with his thumb. Just ahead was a windfall, and a gray wolf was leaping over it to charge straight at him. Another followed, snarling savagely. Link shot twice. The running wolves dropped in their tracks, kicked for a moment, and lay still. Link lowered his rifle, amazed.

He had been completely astonished when, the year before, the black wolf's pack had attacked him. According to the most authoritative reports, North American wolves had never been known to prey on human beings. But the black wolf's pack had been desperately hungry; they had some excuse for acting as they did. How about these?

They must have been mates, with a den under the windfall. Had he approached them on the Gander, they would have remained quiet or slunk away. Wolves would defend their den against almost anything except man, but these wolves had seen so few men that he was just another interloper who must be repelled. Link searched until he found the five squirming pups in the den under the windfall, and did the only thing he could. It was better than letting helpless pups die of slow starvation.

An hour later, Link came to a spring that bubbled up in the spruces, and got down on hands and knees to drink. His eyes were arrested by a depression in the soft earth on the other side of the spring. Link rose to examine it.

It was in soft, dry earth, and the edges had fallen in. But it was not a hoof mark. A prowling grizzly must have left his mark here. Or had he? Link looked away from the track, and again at it. The track was several days old, and crumbled. Its outline was hard to make out, but it seemed oddly elongated for the paw mark of a bear.

Then Link stopped deceiving himself and knew that he was looking at the footprint of a man's boot.

4

Cataract

Link stared perplexedly at the track. It told him nothing except that there was at least one other man in the Caribous. Almost certainly Garridge or Antray had made the track. But where had he gone? He had stepped only once in the soft earth beside the spring, and there was nothing to mark the direction he had taken.

Link bit his lower lip thoughtfully. If Antray and Garridge were still alive, and the track itself seemed evidence that they were, they would be living in a camp or cabin of some sort. Almost certainly it would be near water, probably in a valley. But Antray and Garridge might have decided to camp above timberline, and it would be much to Link's advantage if he stayed there himself, at least for the time being. If there was a camp above timberline he would find it, and from the heights he would have commanding views of the valleys. Should any

55

smoke arise he would be able to see and investigate it. Link looked across the valley below him.

He measured the distance with his eye, and then doubled his mental estimate. Mountain distances were very deceptive; it was entirely possible to look at something that seemed to be a half hour's walk away and then travel six hours before reaching it. Nevertheless, the opposite peaks seemed to be within easy striking distance. Link noted a waterfall that spilled from a snow-capped peak—it would serve as a handy landmark.

It tumbled straight down for a thousand feet or more, a thin stream that pattered over the mountain to jagged rocks far below. Spray floated upward. Link made a mental note of the cataract's location, and went on.

The morning sun climbed higher as he travelled steadily through the high meadows. A little after noon he sat down on a sun-warmed rock to rest. So far he had discovered no further evidence that there were other men in the Caribous. Link glanced back at the cataract, and started in surprise.

He knew he had travelled miles, but the cataract seemed nearly as close as when he had first viewed it. For a moment he thought that his eyes were playing him false. Certainly this could not be the same waterfall. Link studied the landmarks around it and knew that it was.

Only it had undergone a startling change. This

morning a small stream of water had tumbled down the decline, but now a veritable cataract rushed over it. Fierce white water spilled in a misty torrent down the cliff, and Link thought, even at this distance, that he could hear its roar. Amazed, he studied the falls while he sought the reason for its sudden transformation. Then he had the answer.

Every night, in these heights, frost clamped solidly down upon everything and snowstorms were not infrequent. He had first looked at the cataract early this morning. Doubtless it was glacier-fed, and in the early morning it was only a trickle because every night the glaciers froze anew. As the sun became higher, and melted ice and snow, the waterfall gathered volume accordingly. Probably it reached its greatest intensity at high noon and maintained it for two or three hours, until the glaciers again started to freeze.

The cataract was evidence of something else. The Caribous were inaccessible and almost totally unexplored, but there had to be at least one river leading out of them. The water spilled by the cataract, and all the rest of the melting glaciers and snow fields, had to flow somewhere. Link wondered about the river and made a mental note to investigate it. Perhaps it offered a much easier way into and out of the Caribous. But if that were so, why wasn't it known? Almost every northern river that was capable of navigation was mapped from source to

mouth. Of course, the river flowing out of the Caribous might be either too swift or too shallow for
even canoe travel.

Link glanced again into the valleys, and shrugged
his shoulders. Patience, the ability to wait without
fretting, was almost the primary virtue of anything
that lived in the wilds. Small creatures had to wait
many times while a storm abated, or until food was
found, or for some predator to go away. Beasts of
prey waited until they could catch something to eat,
until danger departed, or until weather conditions
permitted them to get where they wished to go.
Link knew how to wait.

Chiri sniffed wistfully at a hot track of some beast
that had passed this way, and looked sideways at
Link. Link grinned understandingly. Chiri had carried his pack for a very long way and had had almost
no free running or any of the hunting he loved to
do. Almost all food brought from the Gander was
eaten. The two packs combined would not now
weigh forty pounds, and Link could carry that easily. He transferred the contents of Chiri's pack to his
own and hung the dog's empty pack on a stunted
tree. He would pick it up if he came back this way
and leave it there if he did not.

Freed, Chiri rolled over and over on the ground,
scratching his back against the rough earth. Then he
sprang up and scampered on ahead. Link walked
on, very conscious of his food problem. Now that he

was far away from the wolf den, game sign was again abundant. He had better replenish his food stores at the first opportunity.

Presently Link stopped in his tracks, and raised his rifle as he saw a mountain sheep standing alertly near a cluster of boulders. Then, recognizing the animal as a ewe, he lowered his rifle.

The ewe both saw and smelled him, but paid no attention. She stood with her head raised, watching the sky. A second later Link saw what she had seen. A golden eagle, at first a far-off dot, was diving down at the ewe with almost bullet speed. Link saw his extended head and talons, then the smooth lines of his feathers as he set his wings and struck.

The ewe met him squarely, rearing on her hind legs, striking with her front feet. The eagle swerved, and rose effortlessly into the air. Link suspected that the ewe was defending her newborn lamb, the real object of the eagle's attack.

The eagle came in again, from a different angle and feinting just before he reached the ewe. He flew on, so near the ground that his wing tips almost touched it, but the ewe refused to take the bait and be lured away. She knew eagles, and understood that, should she get more than a few feet from her lamb, the eagle would double back and kill it before she could return to her baby's defense.

Link watched, fascinated. Golden eagles had all the courage and agility of weasels. When they started a fight they finished it, and when they sought game they got it. The eagle turned and again beat fiercely in. Again the ewe met him, standing on two feet while she struck with her front hooves. The eagle went suddenly limp in mid-air. He tumbled to the ground and did not rise again. One of the ewe's frantic blows had struck exactly the right place.

Rising, the wobbly-legged lamb moved after his mother as she walked away from their fallen enemy. Link made no move. He had no wish to hurt this ewe. She had earned the right to live in her mountain home with her baby.

A half mile farther on Link stopped again, as five grazing deer raised their heads to stare at him. They were bucks, he saw, with velvet-covered bumps of antlers that were just beginning to push through the tops of their heads. Link laid a hand on Chiri's neck, and felt the big dog stiffen. Very gently he stroked the rough fur.

Chiri relaxed and Link raised his rifle. He sighted, squeezed the trigger, and when the gun blasted a buck went down. Link skinned and quartered it, adding the hams to his pack and hanging the front quarters in a tree. It never became warm at this altitude and there were few flies. Meat would keep a long time, and he might be back this way.

Link went down into the timber to make camp. Chiri followed him. Burdenless, frisking ahead, the big dog stopped to dig like an overgrown puppy at a marmot's hole. Then he went off to snuffle through the grass. He offered to molest nothing. There was meat in Link's pack and he knew that when the time came he would share that meat. As long as the next meal was assured, there was no sense in exerting himself to hunt. The future could be taken care of when it arrived.

The next morning they returned to the upland pastures. Link walked in the shadow of the black crags, stopping at intervals to study the valleys and always watching the mountains. The reason for the Caribous' inaccessibility became more and more apparent. They were a ring of rocky mountains surrounding a vast basin of forested valleys. There was one break in that granite wall, the one by which he had entered, but if there was another Link had yet to find it.

When twilight came he descended to the forest again, cut firewood, and made camp. There were the usual snufflings and gruntings, and the shuffle of paws and beat of hooves around the fire, but nothing came in. Obviously the animals in this lost land looked upon fire in much the same light that humans would regard some visible manifestation of black magic. It was fascinating but not understandable, and for that reason better left alone. Link slept soundly near the blaze, satisfied that he would not be molested.

Before dawn he built the fire up, cooked breakfast, and then stamped the fire into the ground. As the sun came up they climbed back to the heights and resumed their circling of the high meadows. With night they returned to timber. Link had discovered nothing. The haze-shrouded valleys had revealed no sign of life; there had been no plume of smoke to mark a camp site, and no visible indications of a wrecked plane. Still, he had seen a footprint, and if he had not discovered Antray's and Garridge's fire it was because something had prevented his seeing it.

He would spend one more day in the heights, Link decided, then descend to the valleys. Maybe the river did offer another way out of the Caribous. Perhaps Antray and Garridge had already gone down it, or were planning to go down. In either event, they should have left some sign of their presence on the river banks.

All the next day Link walked through above-timberline meadows. He found nothing, and shortly before nightfall stopped for a last look into the valleys beneath him. He saw a beaver dam with a white spot near the center, and narrowed his eyes. There was always snow here in the heights, but there should be none in the warm valleys. Then the white spot moved, and Link knew that he was looking at a white moose. The report Antray had heard was true! For a few minutes he stared, intrigued by the first albino moose he had ever seen. Then he looked for Chiri.

The big dog was nowhere in sight.

When Chiri left Link in the heights, it was because he was both curious and unsatisfied. He had spent his entire life in the wilderness, and one of the first things he had learned there was that a hunting animal must know his country thoroughly. He must be aware of the best hunting and hiding places, the most desirable shelters, and of the most advantageous places from which to fight should he be attacked. Not to know all this could mean the difference between life and death.

When he left Link it was with the deliberate intention of going down into the valleys and looking about until he had found what he wanted to know. When he was satisfied he would find Link again. However, instead of starting directly down the slopes, Chiri continued for a while to follow the upland meadows. Once away from Link he slipped easily and naturally back into the ways of a wild thing. When he was with Link, he depended on the man for many things. Alone, he depended only on himself.

Chiri stopped, tail curled over his back while he stared steadily at a herd of white mountain goats that stood on a cliff, pulling lichens from the rocks. A kid reared on its hind legs, turned completely around on a ledge where there did not seem to be enough room for a lizard, danced carelessly for a second, and settled safely on the ledge. Chiri watched, wondering at these sure-footed creatures which could travel swiftly where there was so little foothold.

The herd stared curiously down at Chiri, whom they considered a wolf, and made no moves because they knew that he could not reach them. If goats and sheep were not able to climb out of reach, wolf packs would have exterminated them long ago, and the goats knew it.

After a moment Chiri went on, knowing as well as the goats that he could not climb the cliff, but not caring. He was not hungry. When he wanted food he would be able to find plenty that he could reach. His nose brought him the odor of more goats that were feeding in one of the meadows, as well as the scent of marmots and rock rabbits.

Presently Chiri stopped again. Though it was his intention to go down into the valleys, he had stayed in the high meadows because prevailing winds blew around them. Now the wind had changed and was blowing up from the forest. Chiri caught the odor of moose, black and grizzly bears, and various species of small game. He started down the meadow.

He walked swiftly, keeping his nose in the wind so he could tell exactly what lay ahead of him. He made no special attempt to conceal himself. Though

Chiri had a great respect for some beasts, he feared none. If necessary, he could run away from or fight his way out of any trouble that threatened. Chiri's wonderful staghound legs and Husky endurance had developed to their very peak. He had yet to meet anything able to outrun him and only grizzlies could outfight him.

In the dark forest, an almost black bull moose moved sullenly out of his path. When the dog came near, the moose whirled, backing against a thicket and ready to strike with his front hooves. He inspected the black bull as critically as any human being would, then went on. Probably he could kill the moose; he had pulled bulls down before. But it would take quite a while and he wanted to feed soon. Chiri came to a swift stream, and slunk down beside it.

This, too, was an old game and one he knew well. During his puppyhood he had been able to live partly because of the trout he caught. Big trout, going from one pool to another, frequently broke water with their backs when they swam in shallow riffles. It was possible to pounce on them in such places. But these streams were shallow and swift, almost all riffle, and the trout were not as large as they would be in sluggish streams where there was more food.

Chiri still did not move a muscle, even though there seemed to be no possibility of getting a fish. A squirrel was coming down a spruce within three feet of where he lay. The squirrel stopped, chattering his ill opinion of the world in general. He looked directly at Chiri, but the big dog lay so still that not even his fur rippled. The squirrel came all the way down the tree.

Chiri sprang, snapping his jaws and gulping as he swallowed this tasty morsel whole. It was a mere tidbit, scarcely a mouthful, and Chiri became impatient. Leaping over a log, he blundered among some snowshoe rabbit traces. Because he blundered, and for the time being forgot his hunting skill, he caught nothing. Chiri continued to run.

Suddenly he stopped, and an expression of mischievous delight spread over his face; he had smelled a plodding old porcupine on the ground ahead of him. Chiri had known porcupines since his puppy days, when he had unwittingly poked a friendly nose at one and had it thrust full of quills. Since then porcupines had been strictly on his forbidden list as far as actual contact was concerned, but often they furnished fun.

Chiri began to stalk cat-footedly, making no noise and taking advantage of every particle of cover as he stole forward. He raised his head and shoulders slowly over a fallen log, and in the moonlight saw the porcupine making its fretting way toward a small yellow birch that had found a rooting among the spruces. Protected by the thousand tiny spears he bore on his back and in his tail, serene in his own invincibility, the spiny quill-pig was in no hurry. He had just spent placid weeks gnawing bark from a similar birch a hundred yards from this one, and he wouldn't be hungry for at least twenty-four hours. Time meant nothing to a porcupine, and especially to this one. He was a veteran of the wilderness, an old beast who had not made a swift move in five years.

With a happy whoop Chiri sprang over the log. The porcupine stopped, covering his head with his paws and curling into a round ball that presented only bristling quills to every quarter. Chiri flashed past an inch from the farthest point the quill-pig's snapping tail could reach. Crouching, with his fore-quarters on the ground, he wagged his tail and yapped like a puppy. Around and around the porcupine he flew at full speed, while the spiny, bark-eating beast slapped ineffectively with his tail.

Finally Chiri lay down, panting but happily watching the embattled porcupine. After five minutes the beast lifted his paws, moved his black, oddly beautiful head to every quarter, grunted querulously, and resumed his plodding journey. Chiri, having had his fun and wanting no more, watched his plaything go. The porcupine came to the tree of his choice, gripped with powerful front claws, brought his rear ones up, climbed slowly, and settled in a crotch. He continued to grunt and complain while he washed his face with his front paws.

Forgetting the porcupine, Chiri trotted on. Since leaving Link he had eaten only the squirrel, a morsel that merely teased his appetite. A big dog who needed his strength all the time, Chiri had to have a vast amount of food to keep his body working at the speed which the wilderness demanded. He found the scent of a young moose, followed it a way, and lost it where the moose had entered a small lake to feed on aquatic vegetation. Chiri snuffled about.

He raised his head and moonlight fell glowingly across his mask-like face. Far ahead, he heard a distant murmur. Chiri trotted toward it, knowing as he did so what he would find. He was very familiar with the roar of swift rivers.

This one flowed between tall spruces, a white and angry stream born in distant melting snow banks and glaciers. Wild in its heritage, it had all the turbulence and unrest of mountain country. It was a savage, unnamed thing calmed by no man-made dams.

Chiri accepted the challenge the river flung. He swam into it, breasting the water with all his magnificent strength but still unable to cross. Chiri steered himself deftly around rocks and obstructions, swimming with the snarling current. Three hundred yards down, he emerged on the same side which he had entered.

He shook himself, flinging water in all directions. His tongue lolled happily. Chiri had tried to swim the river for the same reason that he had worried the porcupine; it was a part of the things he knew, a challenge he could not resist. Suddenly he flung his head up.

He had a scent, a faint and far-off wisp of smell that drifted up the river's troubled course. Chiri stood perfectly still, waiting until he could clarify and positively define the scent. When he did, he bristled.

There were two men down the river, two whom Chiri had never smelled before. He stole quietly forward, a drifting ghost in the moon-sprayed night, as he stalked the camp. He wrinkled his nose when the smell of wood smoke became stronger. Chiri stole nearer.

In the soft moonlight, he rounded a tree trunk and looked at the camp. So close, he verified with his eyes the story that his nose had already brought him. Two men lay beside a smoky fire. Unseen and unsuspected, Chiri crept away.

Back in the brush, he trotted swiftly, until he came upon a thicket that reeked of snowshoe rabbit traces. A long-legged, big-footed rabbit flashed ahead of him, and Chiri lengthened out to run. He gained on his fleeing quarry, then overtook it. Chiri snapped once, then lay down to feed. After eating, he sought a warm place beneath a spruce and slept.

Daylight was well advanced when he started out. An errant breeze brought him two strong scents, those of Link Stevens and a bull moose.

5

Meeting

An hour before night fell, Link Stevens went down into the timber. He gathered a great quantity of firewood, arranged his sleeping bag, and built an Indian fire; instead of cutting his wood into fire-sized lengths he laid the ends of a dozen long poles across the blaze. As soon as the ends burned off, the poles could be shoved up. That saved a lot of work.

Link took a strip of rawhide cord from his pocket, dampened it, and tied one end to a haunch of mountain goat he had shot that day. The other end he fastened to a green limb directly over his fire and adjusted the cord until the meat hung just above the searing flames. Twisting the thong, he released it and set the roast to spinning. It wound rapidly in one direction, and its own momentum retwisted the thong. The haunch would turn all night long and be cooked through by morning. While the meat was cooking, Link fried a steak in his skillet, and made a little coffee from his dwindling supply. Then he

71

scrubbed his skillet with a handful of gritty sand, rinsed it, and laid it beside the fire to dry. He leaned comfortably back.

Without Chiri beside him, he had no intention of moving about at night. The meat-eating beasts of the Caribous, wolves, cougars, wolverines, lynx, and bears, seemed to hunt as much by day as by night, but in daylight they could at least be seen. By night they could not. Link already had indisputable evidence that at least some of the predators in the Caribous hadn't the slightest objection to hunting men. Chiri could fend for himself, but Link was glad to stay by the fire.

He moved a couple of burned logs up and watched a shower of sparks float like a swarm of fireflies into the air. He lay down again, watching the sparks wink out, like the eyes of little animals slipping away in the dark. He thought how strange it was that the real personalities of their wild owners were never reflected in night-seen eyes. Caught in a light, a coyote's or wolf's eyes were large and green, like great emeralds. Deer were either red or yellow. Elk and moose reflected dully, like the eyes of a cow. Cats, lynx and cougar, looked as big as saucers and were soft yellow. Rabbits, the most inoffensive of all beasts, had the fiercest eyes. They were little and red, ugly.

Out in the forest a lonesome deer bawled, and there were the usual shufflings and gruntings around the fire. Nothing came near and Link did not look up. He had grown accustomed to all the usual night noises, and soon dropped off to sleep.

He awakened to renew the fire when it burned low. Twice more during the night he arose to build it up, and then it was dawn. Chiri had not returned.

The fire had died to a bed of embers that sent shadowy smoke tendrils skyward. Spinning very slowly, the haunch of meat showed a smoke-blackened crust. Link cut it down, sliced the outer coating away, and revealed perfectly cooked, smoking hot meat. He ate his fill, stowed the rest in his pack, and stared down into the valley where he had seen the white moose.

It wasn't there. Doubtless the moose was back in the forest now, enjoying a nap in the warmth of the spruces. When the sun became warm enough he would come out. If there had been rich and abundant food in last night's feeding place, the moose would probably return there. Link considered.

He had circled above the timberline for days, without seeing even a trace of smoke. Except for the footprint, he had no reason to suppose that the men he was seeking were still alive. His next search would have to be in the forested valleys, but where should he start? Well, the white moose was a clue to his problem, although a poor one. Trigg Antray had come here to see and photograph it. Possibly the moose would somehow lead him to Antray. It was as good a lead as any. Link started down through the forest.

He stepped across an ice-cold little stream that curled among the spruces, and for the first time since getting over the mountains he used his compass. It hadn't been necessary while he stayed in the heights; there he had been able to see where he was going and there had always been landmarks in sight. Here the trees were so big and grew so thickly that he could see almost nothing.

A few minutes later Link hopped across another crystal-clear little stream and paused a moment while he stared at its winding course. There certainly had to be a river flowing out of the Caribous; the cataract and all these little streams must flow somewhere. Just what river did the one arising in these lost mountains flow into? It must be some well-known stream to the east. But which one?

He went on, and presently realized that he was approaching a lake or beaver pond. He smelled a large body of water. Though minutely so, the air was different: it was somehow heavier and wetter. A clump of moose-browsed willows grew in the forest. Link slowed his pace while he searched the forest around him. Two hundred yards farther on, he found both a chain of beaver dams and the white moose.

It stood across a sluggish channel dammed by

beavers, a regal beast of a strange, unreal color. It seemed like a ghost animal, a thing capable of existing only in the wildest imagination. Link blinked his eyes.

Excepting its color, he told himself, this was just another moose, grazing like a barnyard bull. Its muzzle was pink, as were its eyes. It was certainly an albino; even its antlers had a whitish cast. A long streamer of weed clung grotesquely to its antlers as the moose looked around at Link. It stopped chewing to stare.

Link stood perfectly still. At their best, moose were unpredictable. This one might run, or it might seek a closer acquaintance. The bull's mane bristled and its leathery lips rolled back from yellow tushes. It showed no indication of fear. Link beat a hasty retreat, and dodged behind a tree as the moose trotted toward him. Water splashed high under the animal's big hooves. Its trot became a swaying lope.

Link faded farther back into the trees, keeping his rifle ready in the event that it should be needed. He stopped quietly behind a tree, and watched the moose. It halted thirty feet away, grunting and pawing the earth with one ponderous front hoof. Then, with many a backward glance, it returned to the beaver pond. Link skulked quietly away.

At least one portion of the story John Murdock had told him was true; there were albino moose in

the Caribous. Link sighed. If only he could piece
the rest of his problem together, and get back to the
Gander with all the answers! Certainly they were
here to be found, but the Caribous were a big country in which to find anything.

He caught a flicker of motion, a moving gray
shadow in the spruces, and swung his rifle up. Link
rested his thumb on the hammer, ready to cock it.
Then he saw the thing plainly and lowered his rifle.

"Chiri!"

Tail wagging, tongue lolling happily, the big dog
bounded to him and pressed against his thigh. Link
reached down to scratch Chiri's ears, feeling re-
lieved and reassured. In the Caribous there was
never any telling the quarter from which danger
might strike or when it would come, and even the
most alert man could miss seeing it in time. But not
while Chiri was with him. The big dog was keen as a
wolf. No matter what it was or how it tried to stalk
them, he would know and be prepared for it.

Chiri moved a little distance away to snuffle lack-
adaisically at some brush where rabbits had been
playing. Link looked after the departed moose,
shifting his pack to ease a sore spot on his shoulder.
He had found the moose's favorite feeding grounds.
If Antray and Garridge had done the same, where
would they go next? The river? It was as good a
guess as any. He would find the river, and follow it.

Chiri, walking ahead, stopped to drink at a little stream that pitched down a miniature falls into a rock-strewn pool. It was a likely spot for trout. Slipping off his pack, Link took a fishing line from his pocket. He attached a hook, baited it with a chunk of meat, and cast. Almost at once the line tightened and he brought a medium-sized trout up the bank. Link caught another, then three more. He looked at his catch, then at the sun. He had eaten breakfast within the past three hours, but he was hungry again. He gave three of the trout to Chiri, cooked the other two over a small fire, and ate. Link smacked his lips. The trout were flavored only with their own juices, and lacked such products of civilization as salt, pepper, or butter. But Link hadn't seemed to miss them.

They followed the bubbling little stream, and Link watched it critically as he walked. There were a few deep pools and an occasional stretch of still water, but for the most part the stream foamed angrily down steep slopes and pitches. Link shook his head. If the stream was any criterion of what the river would be, then a boat or raft would have trouble on it.

He heard the roar of the river before he came to it, a muted, angry murmur that floated through the spruces, and stopped a moment to listen. Link left the stream to follow a moose path that wound through the spruces. He came suddenly upon the river.

It was wide, three hundred feet from bank to bank. Green spruces lined it. The river, emerald-green, seemed to take its color from their foliage. Obviously it could be forded at this point, for the plainly marked moose trail led up the opposite bank. But it was very doubtful if, even here, anything without the strength of a moose could swim the river or even stand up in it. It seemed gentle at this place only because it was so much swifter above and below. Link looked down the river.

A hundred and fifty feet from where he stood, the river pitched whitely down a riffle. It smashed against a dozen upthrust boulders, and white spray blew high wherever the river hit them. It was true mountain water, a raging, snarling giant, full of trouble and turmoil.

Link had been right. There *was* a river, a big one, flowing out of the Caribous. Whether or not a raft could be taken down it was another matter. If so, it offered a way out. Had Antray and Garridge already tried it?

With Chiri beside him, Link walked down the river's bank. There was little change in the characteristics. Relatively calm pools were fed by tossing rapids, and more white water poured out of the pools and down the next riffles. Link knitted puzzled brows. The riffles seemed shallow. At any rate, the tops of water-lashed boulders jutted through all of them.

Chiri, coursing ahead, halted abruptly. His ruff bristled and a soundless snarl parted his lips. He swung his head to look back inquiringly. Link spoke softly as he advanced to the big dog. He knelt beside him, tickling Chiri's ears with the fingers of one hand while he gripped his rifle with the other. There was something downstream, something that had alarmed the dog. Link held perfectly still, seeking a repetition of an odor that had touched his nostrils for a second and drifted away. Again came the vaguely familiar scent, and this time he pinned it firmly. It was wood smoke!

Chiri padded beside him as Link continued. The smell of smoke strengthened. Chiri stopped again, and Link walked softly through the trees to the edge of a small natural clearing. He halted behind a spruce.

The river roared and thundered here, sending spray high into the air. Beside it, in the clearing, was a rude log shelter, with a fire burning in front of it. The smoke drifting out over the river, mingled with the spray. Link nodded understandingly; no wonder he had been unable to see any sign of smoke from the heights. The river beat it into nothingness.

Two men were sitting beside the fire, cooking

meat over an improvised grill. Both were long-haired and long-bearded, and the clothing they wore had been beaten into tattered rags. Link's eyes were attracted to the smaller of the two men. He sat nearest the fire, attentively watching the meat on the grill. He leaned forward to turn the meat with a long green stick, and glanced silently at his companion. Link turned his eyes to the other man.

He was much bigger, well built and heavily muscled. But he sat motionless, and seemed to be watching his smaller companion furtively. Link thought of a whipped but still sullen Saint Bernard. And, as he dropped a silencing hand to Chiri's head, he decided that both men were a little insane.

Undoubtedly they were Trigg Antray and Thomas Garridge, the men he sought, but the Caribous they thought to conquer had conquered them. It was evident in their actions, in the way they looked at each other, in the tense, almost animal-like air that haunted the camp like a presence. The wilderness, bigger than any one man, had done this before to others. Cabin-fever, some called it, when two good friends isolated themselves in some lonely haunt in the fall and were ready to kill each other before spring came. Others called it bush-madness, a brain fatigue brought on by a constant fight with the wilderness. Neither of the two men beside the fire could be expected to react in any normal way.

Link had found his game. Now how would he bag it? If it was humanly possible, he had to get both these men back to the Gander and turn them over to John Murdock. His task would not be easy.

The simplest course was often the best. Link stepped openly out from behind the tree and walked forward, Chiri beside him.

The smaller man, seeing him first, stared at him in disbelief. Then he rose to his feet. Astonishment was written on his face, but he smiled happily, like a child.

"Dr. Livingstone, I presume?" he said politely.

Link smiled back. "Not quite. My name's Stevens, Link Stevens."

Chiri, walking beside him, bristled and snarled fiercely when the little man came nearer. The stranger stopped, still smiling, and held out his hand.

"My name's Antray, Trigg Antray. And I suppose I don't have to tell you that you're as welcome as flowers in February?"

Link grasped the proffered hand. He tried to maintain his outwardly casual pose while inwardly working on the problems that presented themselves. This smiling little man was unshorn and unkempt, but if he was also insane, certainly no evidence of it was apparent now. Link stole a glance at the second man, still huddling beside the fire but looking steadily at him.

"I hope I didn't startle you!" Link laughed.

"Think nothing of it," Trigg Antray said airily. "I only mind being startled by my sad-faced pal over there. What brings you to this God-forsaken neck of the woods, Link?"

Link remained cautious. "I'm scouting out a new trap-line. Heard there was plenty of game in the Caribous."

"Game there is," Trigg Antray said ruefully. "All sizes, shapes, descriptions, and names. But how did you get here?"

"Through a pass."

Antray looked at him sharply. "Then there is a pass?"

"One that I know of."

"Well, that's one more than I know of. If we'd been able to find a way, we'd have tried to get out of here right after our plane crashed."

"Did either of you get hurt?"

"It didn't do me any good." He lowered his voice and gestured toward the other man. "At that I think I'm better off than he is. Come over and meet Tom Garridge, my pilot. I warn you he isn't very sociable."

Link walked over to meet Garridge, who looked at him from glowering eyes and muttered something Link couldn't understand. Trigg Antray spoke sharply.

"Perk up, old boy. Here's a wandering trapper

who dropped in with his dog. They came through a pass."

Garridge snapped his head around and looked at Link. A new light glowed in his wild, sunken eyes.

"Where's the pass?" he asked hoarsely.

"Quite a ways—across the valley."

"Where?" Garridge insisted.

"Little too far to travel before supper," Link murmured gently. "It lies northeast, right between two twin spires, but there's sort of a tricky trail up to it. You have to climb a high ridge of rock."

"What do the spires look like?"

"Maybe a hundred and fifty feet apart, and sticking a good long way into the sky."

Antray, who had returned to the meat he was cooking, beckoned Link. "Completely off his conk," he said quietly. "He'll be all right as soon as we get him back to civilization. I'm afraid, though, that going through your pass isn't for me. I doubt if I can climb these blasted mountains."

"How badly are you hurt?"

"I don't know; I can't use my lower body effectively. Feel kind of paralyzed from my hips down. But I think we could build a raft and go down this river."

"You think so?" Link's interest was aroused.

"I'm fairly certain; I doubt if the place is as bad as it looks. About three miles down it flows between a high-walled canyon, but it doesn't seem to be too swift there. The problem would be to keep from smashing up on the rocks."

"We'll need a good raft."

"My dear boy, the few brains I possess have been churning to capacity. I have plans which invite your critical inspection, but they can wait until tomorrow. Meantime, you are our guest. If you'll wait a few minutes dinner will be served."

"I have lots of meat."

"Glad to hear it! We haven't much, but you'd better help eat what there is."

Link glanced about the neat camp—Antray did know how to make one—and at the morbid Garridge. Chiri had evidently gone off to hunt.

Antray laid some of his broiled meat on a slab of bark and gave it to Link. Garridge merely glowered at the food brought to him.

"He'll eat when he gets good and ready, and thinks we aren't watching him," Antray said. "I feel sorry for him, but if ever I have to be marooned in the wilderness again I hope it's with somebody who won't blow a fuse."

After they had eaten, Antray yawned and stretched.

"How about it, Link? Can I offer you a private suite in the Hotel Antray?"

Link grinned. "Couldn't stand the luxury. I've been sleeping in the timber so long I'd toss all night if I tried bedding anywhere else. See you in the morning."

"Do that. We're up and around early. You know, early to bed and early to rise—and was that ever a put-up job! If we were wise we wouldn't be here, and if we weren't here we'd be healthy. So we get up early to see what a mess we're in. We'll see you."

Link left the camp and walked back up-river. Out of sight, he cut at right angles, stalked through the trees, and camped on the down-river side. Antray seemed all right in spite of his almost hysterical joking, but Garridge was definitely insane. Until Link found out more about Antray, he'd play a cautious hand.

He built a small fire and lay near it.

6

Suicide River

Link awoke with early dawn. For a few minutes he lay in his sleeping bag, not wanting to move until he knew exactly what was around him. Chiri had not yet returned or, if he had, he had come while Link was asleep and gone away again.

Satisfied that nothing watched him, Link got up quickly, packed his sleeping bag, stamped out his still-smoldering fire, and drifted into the timber. As yet he could be certain of neither Antray nor Garridge. Both might be insane, and if so there was no telling what either would do.

Link considered carefully the facts he had uncovered. Antray, for all his misfortunes, remained bright and cheerful—too cheerful, if anything. But he was certainly not bush-mad. Garridge? Link shook a puzzled head. Obviously he was insane; he seemed unable to think coherently. Until he knew exactly how to handle him, Link decided to remain wary.

He cut through timber to the up-river side of the camp and approached it from the same direction he had left yesterday. As he walked into camp Antray, bending over the fire, hailed him cheerily.

"What ho! I trust you enjoyed a comfortable night?"

"Wonderful!" Link said. "These innerspring mattresses you find all over the Caribous are so soft, and the rooms so well ventilated! How did you find it?"

"Tip-top!" the little man said. "So good, in fact, that old Tom is still asleep." Antray raised his voice. "Tom! We have a guest for breakfast!"

There was no answer from the log shelter. Antray looked at Link.

"Poor devil! Well, at least he isn't thinking while he's sleeping, though I wouldn't care to have his dreams. A few weeks of rest may fix him up, but first we have to get him back to civilization. That seems to be a bit of a job."

"How long has he been this way?"

"Since the day our plane crashed. He screamed at the top of his voice all the while we were coming down. Hasn't been right since."

"Has he given you any trouble?"

"He hasn't been violent, if that's what you mean, and he seems willing enough to do all he can. But he's completely off his rocker and he's been getting steadily worse."

"Has he been away from you for any length of time?"

Antray frowned. "He's done almost all the hunting; if he hadn't I don't know what we would have lived on because I haven't been able to hunt. Tom's killed our game for us, and I smoked as much as I could because I knew we didn't have an endless store of cartridges. All we managed to salvage was one box. They played out sooner than I thought. Two weeks ago Tom came back with part of a caribou—and an empty rifle. I sent him after the rest of the caribou and smoked it. That was our supper last night, and if it seemed a bit 'high' who are we to complain? Gourmets like it that way. I've been trying to piece out with fish."

"You got any grub at all?"

"My dear Link, in a very literal sense we are living from river to mouth. The food we have in reserve, believe me, would not nourish a deer mouse."

Link nodded. Everything was adding up as it should. Doubtless Garridge, looking for game and possibly also searching for a pass, had left the single footprint. Insane though he might be, Garridge evidently knew how to get along in the wilds. He had probably sunk to his present condition only after their ammunition had given out and he could no longer hunt.

"How did you two ever land here?" Link asked.

Antray laughed. "That's a long, sad story, Link. I've done a bit of lecturing here and there, and I like to illustrate my little talks with colored movies. I heard about the Caribous from an Indian named Pinebranch, so last fall I flew over here with Slim Hendryx, and Slim brought me down for a look.

"I saw an albino moose, as far as I know the only one anybody's ever seen. Presto! Opportunity was practically kicking me in the face. I decided that I needed a closer look at the moose and, if possible, some colored movies of it. Then I could climb back on my little lecture stand with brand new material.

"I tried to get Slim Hendryx to bring me back into the Caribous, but Slim was busy so I hired Garridge. I didn't know him, but he said he was an experienced bush pilot and that was enough. Most of these bush pilots could put wings on an orange crate, use a rubber band to spin their propeller, and go anywhere."

"So I've heard. What happened?"

"I doubt if it was Garridge's fault, but after one swing over the mountains the plane lost headway. At the same time, Garridge lost his head. We landed in a little lake about a mile from here, and the plane floated only long enough to let us grab the rifle and cartridges, a couple of knives, some emergency rations, and a box of waterproof matches. So, here we are."

Link opened his mouth to speak, but just then Garridge crawled out of the log shelter.

He came slowly, sullenly, looking at Link and Antray out of the corners of his eyes. Again Link thought of a whipped and sullen dog. Garridge seemed too beaten to care what happened. Except for his momentary interest in the pass the night before, he had not spoken one word since Link had arrived.

Antray turned to Link, as if continuing a previous conversation.

"Find enough fur sign to interest you?"

"Plenty."

"Are you going to winter here?"

"I hope to."

"Br-r!" Antray said. "You're a better man than I am, then. I'm supposed to be an outdoorsman, but I wouldn't winter here, if I could help it, for a king's ransom in fur. Do you have your supplies in?"

"Not yet. I'm going back for them."

"Now you're making skookum talk!" Antray cried. "I don't suppose the prospect will fill you with joy, but how about taking Tom and me with you when you go?"

Link nodded. "Sure thing, and we'd better make it as soon as possible. But I thought you said you can't climb?"

"I doubt it. How about the river?" Antray asked eagerly. "I know it looks bad, but I doubt if it's as bad as it looks. I've been stuck here long enough to know. The danger lies in the rocks that thrust up through the rapids, but I'm sure three of us can steer a raft around them. Tom will help and he's strong as a bear. I've already sent a small raft down and, though I couldn't keep it in sight, I know it got through at least as far as the canyon."

"That the canyon you were telling me about?"

"Yes. The river flows between high walls there, but it doesn't look too swift. Incidentally, those blasted walls are the only reason we can't walk out. There just isn't any place to walk. It will be better for me, anyway, if we can depend on water all the way, down to some river we know. I think we can do it."

"Let's eat and then figure things out."

"Right," Antray agreed. "First things first."

Link sliced the remainder of his haunch of roasted goat meat, gave Antray some, and laid a share for Garridge on a strip of birch back. Garridge shrank back when he came near, but reached out and gobbled the meat as soon as he turned away.

Antray had his mouth stuffed full and was chewing happily.

"A lot of men would be dead if they couldn't live exclusively on meat," he observed, "though I'm going to eat nothing but vegetables and fruit for sixty-five years after I get out of here. Where's your big dog, Link?"

"Out somewhere. He hunts for himself."

"Good dog, eh?"

"The best."

Antray finished eating and fastidiously wiped his hands on a bit of grass. Then he stood up and turned to Link.

"Come on," he said eagerly. "Let's go down and have a look at the river."

Antray set off down the river bank, a place with which he was obviously familiar. Link walked close behind him. Garridge, saying nothing and maintaining a safe distance between Link and himself, brought up the rear. They walked slowly, dodging around trees and following various paths along the bank. Link studied the river.

It was much as it had been above. Swift pools were fed by angry riffles, and in turn spilled into the next pool. Link studied the rocks in the riffles carefully. It was true that white water often looked worse than it was, and possibly experts could take a canoe down this river—if they had a canoe. A raft could not possibly descend without hitting some rocks, but if it were made strongly enough it would weather some bumps and crashes. A good steersman could help a lot.

Link drew up behind Trigg Antray, who was standing on a smooth boulder that overhung swift water. Garridge stayed behind. A hundred and fifty feet downstream the river purred between two rock walls, massive granite monuments that rose a thousand feet into the air. Perfectly smooth, they did not seem to offer a foothold for even a mountain goat. A single rock-studded riffle broke the river's even flow through the canyon.

Antray turned to Link. "What do you think?"

"It'll be a good trick if we can do it."

"Don't you think we can?"

"It looks bad."

Antray's face fell.

"I don't say it can't be done," Link said. "Can you handle a steering pole?"

"Yes. There's nothing wrong with my arms. It's the rest of me that needs some reconditioning."

"How far can we depend on Garridge?"

Antray shrugged. "You've seen Tom yourself. You know how he is—licked, but still strong as a bull."

"You said he's willing to help."

"What are you driving at?"

"Just this. I don't like the looks of your river and I don't aim to drown in it. But rivers often look worse than they are, and I've got a hundred feet of rope. If we could try running a couple of these riffles, but at the same time stayed pretty sure that we could get back if we failed, it might work out. Would Garridge haul us in if we needed it?"

"I get you!" Antray exclaimed. "You mean we're going to test-hop some of the riffles, with a sort of safety anchor if we should find we can't do it?"

"That's about the size of things."

"If you'll leave Garridge to me, he'll do anything I say."

About to speak, Link changed his mind. Looking at Garridge, he could see nothing to prove that he would not take orders. Garridge's abject air, and his apathy, were natural results of his twisted mentality. Link looked doubtfully at the river. It was a lot to risk, with nobody except an unbalanced man to offer them assistance should they fail. But if he tried it at all he needed Antray on a steering pole. Besides, Antray had said that he could handle Garridge—and there was no assurance that they would fail. Even if they could not run the riffles and Garridge proved undependable, probably he and Antray could save themselves. At any rate, the advantages to be gained if they proved they could run the river outweighed the risks they must take. Link turned to Antray.

"Let's go back and build a raft."

Antray grinned his delight. "Right-o, old boy. But all we really need do is go back and finish a raft."

"What do you mean?"

"I will demonstrate. Follow me, and you shall see that I have not been idle. I told you I had plans."

Antray led the way back up-river, and turned aside a hundred yards from the camp to limp through a thick growth of small trees. Link followed, to emerge again on the bank at a relatively quiet pool. He looked wonderingly at the great heap of ashes there, and at the large pile of logs.

They were dead pine, light and buoyant stuff with no wet or heavy centers, and they had been burned at both ends until they were almost a uniform length of about fourteen feet. A foot from either end, and again in the center, each log was pierced by a charred hole about two inches in diameter. Link looked at Antray, and voiced his amazement.

"You must have spent weeks doing this!"

"Time, my friend, was one thing I had plenty of. And how was I to know that divine providence was to direct your wandering steps hither? I burned the logs to an even length and floated them down to here." Antray reached down to pick up a ten-foot section of tough wild grapevine. "This was my rope. I figured that if it did not break while I was holding onto a log in this swift river, it would help hold the raft together."

"How did you put the holes through the logs?"

Antray shrugged. "An elementary law of science, Link, one known for thousands of years. Still, in all truth, I had to re-discover it for myself. I told you that Tom brought a useless rifle back to camp. I heated the barrel and burned the holes."

Link shook his head in wonder. "How did you intend to hold it together?"

Antray entered the brush, prowled about for a moment, and emerged with a stick which he had whittled until it was two inches in diameter by eight feet long. He thrust an end into one of the charred holes, and Link noted with approval that it made a tolerable fit.

"Another spur-of-the-moment invention. I have three of these pegs to drive through the holes, and I thought I would bind the raft together with vines."

"What if the vines broke?"

"It would have been an indication that they were not strong enough."

Link grinned. Antray, who did not even pretend to be a practical woodsman, alone and hurt in the wildest possible land, had still planned his own salvation intelligently. There was no denying his ingenuity and courage. But the raft could be improved. Link set to work with his axe, splitting some of the logs by driving wooden wedges into them.

Chiri, well-fed and satisfied, slunk out of the forest to steer a wide berth around Antray. He sat down near Link's rifle, and when Antray came near Chiri drifted silently away. Trigg Antray looked quizzically at Link.

"Your dog doesn't seem to trust me."

"He doesn't trust anybody."

Link fitted the logs together, using the axe blade to smooth their sides, then drove Antray's pegs through the holes. That done, he cut two eight-foot sections of rope, unravelled them to double their length, and tied them around the raft. Meantime, Antray had cut two long pushing poles. Using one as a lever, they pried the raft's front end two feet off the ground, then let it drop. The raft remained solid. They raised and dropped the rear end.

Link wiped the perspiration from his face.

"There! She ought to take some bumps."

"Looks strong enough to go over Niagara Falls," Antray agreed. "What now?"

Link looked at the lowering sun. "Let's call it a day and make an early morning start tomorrow. Right now, I'm hungry."

"So am I," said Antray. "You've done the work so I'll provide the dinner. What do you prefer?"

Link grinned. "Fried chicken with a peck each of green onions, lettuce, and tomatoes on the side."

"We're just out of them," Antray said, "but I can recommend the bull trout. It's strictly fresh—in fact, not even caught yet."

"All right, but I think the Hotel Antray offers mighty poor service."

Antray produced a fish line and hook, baited with a chunk of meat, and walked down to the river.

Twenty minutes later he was back with a supply of trout. Expertly he filleted and broiled them. After they had eaten he looked at Link.

"Going to sleep in the forest again, wild man?"

"I reckon."

Antray smiled. "I know that neither Tom nor I are exactly models of elegance, but we have had an occasional bath. Is there some other reason why you shun our company?"

"It's," Link fumbled for a reason, "it's my dog. He won't stay if there's anyone else around and I want him back."

"Oh. I see."

Antray appeared satisfied with the explanation, but Link felt a little ashamed. The whole situation was clear enough; Antray was sound as a nut, and Garridge was too sunk in despair to be dangerous. Still, everything was going smoothly enough. It was best to leave it that way.

But Chiri did not come in to his lonely fire, and with the first streaks of early dawn Link reappeared at the camp alone. Garridge sat with his back against the side of the log shelter, his head buried in his hands. Antray looked up from the fire.

"Ah, voyager!"

"Hi, I reckon this is the morning."

"Definitely. We'll soon know whether or not we can escape our prison via the river route."

Garridge raised his shaggy head and stared dully

at Link. Antray turned the fish he was broiling on the grill.

"Never again claim that we do not offer a varied fare," he jibed. "This morning it's grayling."

"Wonderful!"

Link ate, and walked down to look once more at the river. The rocks in the riffles looked even higher and more dangerous than they had the day before. He returned to the camp and glanced questioningly at Garridge.

"Is everything all right?" he asked Antray.

"Right as rain, old boy. Tom knows what he's supposed to do and is ready to do it."

Link tied one end of his coil of rope to the raft and stood expectantly, holding the coil. Accompanied by Garridge, Trigg Antray limped down to the river. He turned to his companion, and spoke slowly, as though Garridge were a child.

"We aren't running away from you, Tom. You can depend on that. All we want to find out is whether or not we can run these riffles. If we can, we'll know that we can get all the way down the river. Then we'll be back home, Tom, home! Remember, if we get in trouble snub the rope around the first tree you can reach. If we raise a hand, snub it anyway. Understand?"

Garridge nodded dumbly. Trigg Antray picked up one of the two long pushing poles and Link took the other. Using the two poles as levers, they pried the raft out into the river. Garridge leaned back on the rope, not seeming to exert all his strength but holding the raft steady. Antray turned to Link.

"Think we should shed some clothes?"

"It wouldn't be a bad idea. It's easier to swim without a water-logged jacket than it is with one."

Antray threw his jacket down on the bank. Link dropped his beside it and stepped out on the raft. It bobbed under his weight but did not sink appreciably. Antray followed him, and deliberately walked to the off-bank side. There was nothing wrong with the little man's courage. Should there be an accident, the man nearest the bank would have a much better chance of gaining safety. Link turned to him.

"All set?"

"Right-o."

Link sank his pole into the river bed and pushed the raft out. Garridge, who seemed to understand his duties and responsibility perfectly, paid out rope. The raft gathered speed as it entered the first riffle. Link stood with knees bent, ready with his pole. Skillfully he fended the raft from an exposed rock and waited for the next one. He looked at Garridge, following them down the bank, apparently alert. When the raft bobbed suddenly toward the shore, he knew that Antray had pushed it away from a rock on his side. Antray, too, seemed to know exactly what he was doing.

Some of Link's nervous tension ebbed away.
Evidently Antray knew his rivers; he had said that a
raft could run this one, and maybe he was right.
Link shoved the raft away from the rock near the
shore. Then they were into the next pool, through
it, and into the next riffle.

It was much swifter and stronger than the first
had been. White water foamed all about. Link kept
his pole constantly busy, pushing the raft away from
protruding rocks, and Antray was as busy as he.
Then disaster loomed suddenly.

Just ahead the river broke over a whole row of
toothed rocks jutting unevenly through the water.
The raft could not possibly miss them; there was
scarcely room for a swimming otter to pass between
that array of boulders. Link raised his right hand,
signalling for Garridge to snub the raft, and braced
himself for the expected shock. When it did not
come he risked a shoreward glance. His heart sank
to his boots.

Garridge was no longer there! The snubbing rope
trailed uselessly in the water as the raft bore down
on the rocks. Link stole a glimpse at Antray, who
had also seen the danger and was readying himself
for it.

White water swirled around them as the raft was
cast high up on the rocks. Casting his pushing pole
as far as he could, Link rode with the shock. He
tumbled over the end of the raft into the icy water,

feeling for the rope as he fell. He grasped it and let himself be whirled downstream by the current. He did not try to fight as the water rolled him over and over.

Link brought up with a sudden jerk, and he knew that the rope had tightened against the stranded raft. Then it loosened and again he was whirled downstream; the raft had ridden over the rocks. Link still swam with the river, fighting to hold onto the rope and to keep his head above water. He passed under a water-touching spruce branch, and snatched at it with his free hand, clinging desperately.

Water roared in his ears, and it seemed that he could no longer see well, but he knew that he had to work fast. Link drew himself up, snubbing the rope around the branch he had grasped. The branch bent sharply down-river as the raft came to a sudden violent stop and swung in to shore. Link tied the rope, and hand over hand drew himself along the branch to the river's bank.

For a moment he lay gasping, but there were things to be done. Link made himself get up, and staggered to the raft. He saw Antray clinging to it, and threw himself prone. Link's hands encircled the little man's wrists.

With a mighty effort he pulled Trigg Antray onto the raft.

7

Left to Die

For ten minutes they lay side by side on the raft, gasping for breath which the icy shock had taken from them. Antray closed his eyes, lapsed into semiconsciousness. Link stood up and staggered to the river's bank. He half-fell, forced himself to stand, and then felt better. Strength seemed to flow back into his legs and his head was clear.

"Antray!" he called.

Trigg Antray stirred feebly, then rolled completely over and raised his head. Making a valiant effort, he pushed himself up with his forearms. Still weak, but stronger than he had been, Link walked across the raft to help him. He knelt to pass his arms around the other's shoulders.

"Get up!" he shouted. "We can't stay here!"

Antray's voice was a whisper. "I—I'm coming, old chap!"

Antray rose to his hands and knees, and then to his feet as Link kept supporting arms around his shoulders. The little man stumbled, almost went down, and then he, too, seemed to regain his strength. He sat down on the river bank and for a moment buried his face in his hands. Retching violently, he spat out a great quantity of water. Some color flowed back into his face. He smiled wanly.

"I'm sorry, Link."

"What about?"

"Thought sure I could trust the bounder."

"Shucks, we needed a bath anyway."

Unquestionably Antray was telling the truth. If he hadn't thought he could trust Garridge, he never would have gotten on the raft himself. He could scarcely be blamed for what had happened, but both of them were fools, Link told himself, for placing any confidence at all in Garridge. Well, they had tried it and failed, and there was no sense in crying about it.

"Can you walk?" Link asked.

"Give me a couple of minutes."

"Sure."

"I wonder," Antray speculated, "what the devil ever possessed Tom to let go of that rope?"

"Couldn't hold it," Link answered, "or maybe he's blown his top completely."

"You're probably right. Well, let's go back and see what he can say for himself. If he wasn't off balance I myself would beat him to a pulp with the first club I could find."

"Well, let's go back and find out," Link said.

Travelling slowly and obviously in pain, Antray led the way up the river's bank. Link, who felt almost his old self, waited patiently while the little man rested. His admiration for Antray increased. He was badly hurt and he knew it, but he would ask neither help nor pity. There was nothing wrong with his fighting heart.

Antray stopped to rest just short of the camp, while a whiskeyjack in a tree overhead chuckled hoarsely at them. Link looked up the river, vaguely troubled by a presentiment that all was not well. He did not know why he felt that way, but there was something in the air, like the tension that precedes a thunderstorm.

"I think I'll go ahead," he suggested, "just to make sure everything's all right."

"What can be more wrong than it is?"

"I don't know, but I aim to find out."

Link slipped past Antray, and trotted up the river bank. He came to the camp, and stopped short. His blood seemed to freeze in his veins.

Garridge was not there, and neither, as far as Link could see, was anything else except the shelter. Link's eyes darted to the place where he had left his rifle; the space was empty now. He and

Antray were deserted in the Caribous with the clothes they wore and whatever might be in their pockets. Even their jackets were gone, stolen by the insane Garridge. Link tried futilely to consider all the connotations of their terrible predicament.

For the moment he was unable to think clearly at all. He knew only that man was supreme in the wilds for two reasons: the weapons he carried and his ability to reason. Otherwise he was no match at all for the savage wilderness. Link's trance was broken by Antray's quiet voice.

"He took everything he might need, didn't he?"

Link continued to stare at the ravaged camp. Suddenly he strode forward to bend down and look into the log shelter. It was no use. Everything was gone. Antray tried to control his chattering teeth.

"Well," he said, "let's build up the fire and get warm, anyway."

He picked up a dried stick and poked about in the ashes of the cooking fire. He straightened, his face ashen-gray. His words seemed slow and labored.

"Even an insane man wouldn't do that."

"What?"

"Link, he's thrown water on the fire. There isn't even a spark left."

Link searched his wet pockets desperately. "My matches were in my jacket," he said hoarsely. "How about you?"

The little man shook his head. "I'll run down to

the store and get some," he said sardonically. "Anything else?"

The words sounded fanciful, unreal. Matches were one of the commonest articles; everyone took them for granted and was never without them. Of course nobody could be without them. They meant heat, cooking fires, safety, life itself! Link swallowed hard, and looked grimly at Antray.

"Do you suppose he wanted to kill us? Did he let go of the rope hoping we'd drown?"

"I wouldn't believe that of any man!"

"I would. If he was just skipping with my equipment, why did he put out the fire?"

"I guess you're right. How long will it take us to reach the pass you spoke of?"

"We'll never live to get there. Where do you think we are, in a park?"

"If I may say so, there doesn't seem to be much possibility of our continuing to live here."

"We'll make out, but it will take some planning."

"The dauntless trapper," Antray murmured. "How long will it take dear old Tom to reach the pass?"

"Several days at least. All he knows is the general direction. We have to catch him before he reaches it."

"How? As you pointed out, this is rather unfriendly country to travel in, without fire or weapons."

"Let's take an inventory," Link suggested.

Antray patted his pockets. "I'm afraid I can contribute little to the stock pile. I pretty well stripped myself before I started out on our accursed raft."

He felt in his pockets, bringing out two buttons, a water-soaked notebook, the stub of a pencil, and an extra hank of fish line. Link sank his hands in his own pockets, but he, too, had transferred almost everything to his jacket before starting out on the raft. He produced his compass, which was still in working order, and a stag-handled jackknife with the smaller blade broken.

"What ho!" Antray said with grim humor. "We're armed!"

"We'd better be, and soon."

Link stepped to a grove of aspens, and selected a straight tree about two and a half inches in diameter. He leaped to catch the trunk farther up, and climbed higher. The tree swayed, and bent under his weight. Link ascended still higher, and the top of the tree bent farther. Link kicked his legs out, clinging to the tree with both hands, as it bent toward the earth. Link's feet touched the ground. Hand over hand he worked his way along the trunk until he was gripping it near the tip. The tree bent in an arc, with the leafy top brushing the earth. Link called over his shoulder.

"You hold her down while I cut."

"Right-o!"

Antray seated himself among the topmost branches, holding the tree where it was while Link went to work on the trunk. It was always easier to cut green wood when it was under tension, and aspen was one of the easiest woods to cut. Even so, the tree was no simple thing to cut with a jackknife. Finally the tree snapped, leaving a long strip of ragged bark clinging to the severed stump. Link hacked out a length of wood about three feet long. He trimmed it and shaved a handhold, then fashioned another three-foot club for Antray. The little man swished his through the air.

"Superb!" he announced admiringly. "Just like movie cave men!"

Link was irritated. "It's no laughing matter."

"I could lie down and scream," Antray suggested mildly. "Do you think that would be more helpful?"

Link grinned his apology. "I'm sorry. I just let myself get keyed up."

"That won't help either, old boy," Antray told him. "I assure you it won't. If we're going to get out of this blasted mess, we'll need every weapon we have and our own perspective is one of them. Let's keep it."

"I agree."

Link swung his own club, getting the feel of the weapon in his hands. Suddenly he thought of that other hunter, the man who had prowled the mountains and had left his arrow embedded in the grizzly. Even he had been provided with more of the tools necessary for survival than Link and Antray now possessed. He had had a bow and arrow, and beyond any doubt he had had fire. But they had not been enough. Link moistened dry lips with his tongue.

"Do you know anything about primitive fire-making?"

Antray shook his head. "An art I never mastered, Link. Never thought I'd need it. I used a match for all the wood fires I ever started. I can try it but I won't guarantee to produce a blaze."

"We'd better try."

Link knew that there were beasts in the Caribous just as willing to hunt and eat men as anything else, and that only fire would keep them away. He searched about for a dead tree, and when he found one he pried a long strip of dead wood from its outer trunk. He broke the slab across his knee, so that he had two chunks of almost equal size, and used the point of his knife to drill a small hole into but not through each. Antray interrupted him with forced calmness.

"We seem to have a visitor."

Link dropped the two pieces of wood, but instinctively retained the grip on his knife as he sprang erect. Not thirty paces away, a gray timber wolf was looking speculatively at them. Link clutched the knife more tightly, and realized what a puny, totally inadequate weapon it was. Only then did he think of the club, and stooped to pick it up. When he straightened, the wolf was gone.

"He wasn't hungry," Antray said with relief, "or perhaps we looked too tough to chew."

Link nodded as he swung the club. He would have to condition himself to an entirely new way of thinking, and to react quicker. When Antray warned him, so new was the weapon and so foreign the idea of using it, he hadn't even thought of the club, which was a far better weapon than the knife. He had merely felt helpless and thwarted because he hadn't a rifle in his hands. Well, he had no rifle and he might just as well get used to the idea. Link stooped to pick up his two pieces of dead wood.

"Keep your eyes peeled," he admonished. "Our little pal might be back."

"Hope I see him first," Antray said.

Though he had to exert a conscious effort to do so, Link leaned his club beside him while he finished working the two pieces of wood. He had always thought he knew thoroughly the old wilderness rule that eternal vigilance is the price of life. But now he had to amend it. Eternal vigilance plus split-second reaction was the price of life in the Caribous. One error would almost certainly be one too many. The visiting wolf probably was hunting meat, and if there had been another wolf with him, they might have tried to get it where they found it.

Link cut a limber branch from the felled aspen, found a foot-long straight stick, and sat down to unlace one of his trail boots. Never once had he started, or even tried to start, a fire by friction and he had only dim hopes of succeeding now. But he knew of nothing else he could try. Link strung the rawhide shoe lace loosely across the limber stick, caught his straight stick in a roll of the lace, and put one end of the stick in the hole on the bottom piece of dead wood. Carefully, selecting the finest and driest bits of tinder he could find, he arranged them around the hole. Then he pulled the fire-stick erect, placed his remaining slab of dead wood over it, and worked the improvised bow back and forth.

The fire-stick whirled, but nothing else happened. After fifteen minutes, when Link felt the tinder, it was only slightly warm. He rose, then bent to pick up his club while he tried to puzzle out what he had done wrong. According to theory he should have had a fire before this.

"Do you think your fire-stick's too green?" Antray asked.

"It might be. Wish we'd brought a Boy Scout along."

"Suppose you let me try, while you take the wolf watch. After all, waiting for a man-eating wolf to come along can become monotonous. I think we need a fair division of labor."

Antray walked to a spruce and broke off one of the

dead lower branches. He dismembered it with his hands, selected a stick that would fit the holes in the two slabs, and put it in place. He whirled it, and the stick broke. The little man selected another stick, and set to work again. A wisp of smoke arose from the tinder and Antray knelt to blow it gently. Then, after a hopeful moment, the bit of smoke died away. Antray shredded more tinder and patiently put it in place.

For half an hour he worked steadily, keeping just enough tension so the fire-stick would not break. When he finally did look up his face was wan, drawn, and for the first time there was a hint of discouragement in it. But he still smiled.

"If you want to know what I think, I think there are better ways of starting fires."

There was a sudden rattle of wings, and a spruce grouse lit in a tree ten feet away. Antray froze where he was. Link took a cautious step forward while the hen clucked curiously at him. He drew his club back slowly, scarcely daring to breathe as he turned his eyes away from the bird. There was a theory which Link had never proven or disproven, that nothing could alarm wild things quite so much as the steady stare of something else. He felt sweat break on his forehead.

He controlled a wild impulse that bade him leap at the bird, to hurl his club before he was ready, to do anything that might have the remotest chance of getting food. At the same time, he wondered about his control. Did man, shorn of his civilized trappings, become instinctive? He wanted to rush at the bird but something held him back, something he had never felt before. This must be the way a wolf felt when it stalked a deer, or a weasel when it hunted a squirrel. Perhaps all hunting beasts looked and felt tense because they had an urge to spring long before they were ready, and maybe only the grim necessity for survival controlled that urge. Link knew only that he wanted to hurl his club and didn't.

He took another step toward the hen, and another, until the bird sat straight upright. It looked at him with bright, beady black eyes, and made ready to fly. Just as the grouse spread its wings, Link hurled his club.

He stopped, waiting breathlessly. The bird was almost in the air when the club struck it squarely. The green branches swayed as the grouse fluttered frantically among them. Then it dropped to the ground. Link sprang forward, making a tackle that pinned the grouse beneath his chest. He felt for the downed bird with his hands, and gave a quick twist to its neck.

The feeling of tension passed and was replaced by a sensation of confidence. Gone was the cold fear that had swept over him when he saw the plundered camp. He knew now that it was by no means a foregone conclusion that he and Antray would die. They had failed to make a fire, but they had faced a prowling wolf, and he had brought down game. The applied intelligence of a human being might yet triumph over anything which this Stone Age wilderness could pit against it. Link remembered to recover his club, which had fallen beside the grouse. Then he stood up, holding the dead bird by its neck.

"That," Antray said, "was a spectacle."

"Now *I* feel like a cave man," grinned Link.

Link skinned the bird, breaking the wings at their upper joints and smoothing the pile of feathers carefully. He dressed the grouse with his knife, laying even the head and entrails carefully on one of the slabs of dead wood with which he had tried to start the fire. Antray looked curiously at them.

"Waste not, want not," he quoted. "Why are you saving the offal?"

"Figure we may use it."

Antray grimaced. "I'm not that hungry."

"Not yet, you mean."

"Well, maybe not yet."

Link sat down on the river bank, staring across the rushing water as he tried to think. Night was coming on, and with it he and Antray would be at the mercy of any prowling beast that cared to hunt them. They couldn't be safe beside a fire when they had no fire and no means of starting any. They might conceivably have a chance if Chiri were there to warn them. But Chiri was still prowling the wilderness. Link turned to Antray.

"I'm just about stumped. Have *you* got any ideas?"

"On what subject?"

"On keeping alive through the night."

"Climb a tree and spend the night in it."

"No good. Cats can climb trees, and there's both cougar and lynx here in the mountains. A lynx wouldn't bother us, but . . ."

Link left his sentence half finished. A cougar shouldn't bother them, either, but high in the pass was a cougar's den with the skeleton of a man in it. They were facing fact, and not what somebody who had never been in such a predicament considered fact. Again Link let his eyes wander over the river. There was something there, something that should be translated into safety for them, but he seemed unable to think of it.

"We can't eliminate all risk, but we can cut it down. What we should have is a couple of lances."

"Oh sure, or a suit of armor!"

"I'm not fooling," Antray protested. "I don't mean the sort King Arthur used, but at least we can have as good a lance as his ancestors carried. Then, if we have to defend ourselves, we won't have to wait until the blasted beast gets near enough to use these clubs. I think we can cut a couple of slender aspens and contrive some sort of point on them."

Link looked appreciatively at the little man. Trigg Antray probably was afraid, but he did not show it and his suggestion was practical. At best a pointed stick was a crude instrument.

"Good idea," he admitted.

He walked to a dense growth of aspens and pushed through them to the crowded center, where trees grew very slender and tall. Link selected two, cut them, and trimmed the branches until he had two ten-foot poles that tapered from three quarters of an inch in diameter at their small ends to an inch at the large. He shaved points on them.

"Have at thee, knave!" Antray cried.

The little man balanced his lance in a melodramatic pose and sparred with an imaginary foe. Link grinned, but the value of the lances was very apparent, all the same. Any attacking beast could be met at ten feet, and could at least be wounded before close-up work with clubs was necessary.

Link glanced ruefully at his knife, whose blade had become dull, and walked down to the river. Selecting a smooth stone, he carefully honed a keen edge onto the knife. Tattered, bearded, and long-haired, Antray knelt beside him. Link looked up, wondering if he were the same way. He glanced at the river.

"I've got it! The raft! We'll spend the night there!"

Carrying his lance and club in one hand, and the grouse and refuse in the other, Link led the way down the river. They met a cow moose that stamped an impatient foot and stood her ground for a moment. Link balanced his lance, ready to receive her charge should one come, and Antray moved up beside him. But the cow changed her mind, whirled, and went back into the forest.

They reached the raft, still tugging at the branch to which Link had tied it. For a moment Link studied the situation, then he laid the grouse on the ground and handed his club and spear to Antray.

"Hang onto my arsenal and keep your eyes open," he instructed. "I'm going to ease her down into quieter water."

Link loosened the line, being careful to retain a half hitch over the branch, and let that slip carefully. When the raft was finally freed, he could hold it. Foot by foot he floated it down-river into a quiet pool. Link snubbed the raft around a tree, and drew it in until only about twenty feet of rope extended into the river. He cut another fifteen feet from the other end of the rope and hunted along the river bank until he found a heavy, oblong boulder. Lashing one end of his rope to that, he carried the boulder to the stern of the raft and tied the free end. Antray was skeptical.

"I get the idea. If anything comes tonight you're

going to whirl that little stone around your head and knock its brains out."

"Wrong."

Link found a dead pole, and kicked the branches off with his feet. He laid his lance, club, the grouse, and the grouse's head and entrails, on the raft and poised with his pushing pole. A few hundred feet back in the forest, something grunted.

"Better get aboard," Link said. "Whatever that is might decide to pay us a visit."

Antray hesitated a moment, then said, "I still don't know what you're planning, but I'll come along."

He got on the raft and Link issued his instructions: "As soon as I get us out into the stream, push the anchor off."

Link plunged his pole into the river and shoved powerfully. The raft moved away from the bank and out into the pool. Link sank his pushing pole on the down-stream side to hold it there. Antray shoved the boulder into the river and Link pulled up his pole. The raft swept five feet downstream and stopped, with at least four yards of open water, spanned only by the taut rope, between it and the shore.

"As safe," Link said cheerfully, "as we would be in church!"

8
Vigil

Riding high in the water, the raft rocked gently as the current purled against it. It began to grow dusk. A silver-tipped grizzly walked out on the river's bank a few yards from the tethering rope and stood with all four feet braced. He swung his huge head toward them, and his tongue lolled as he looked at the two on the moored raft. Without hesitation the grizzly walked down to the river and drank. He stood with his front paws in the water, staring at the raft, and Link involuntarily grasped his lance with both hands while sweat broke out on his forehead. Then, unhurriedly, the grizzly walked back into the forest, stopping to turn again before he finally disappeared. Antray was badly shaken.

"Whew! Friendly cuss, what? There were a few seconds when I thought he'd like to spend the night with us!"

"Don't be afraid of a little grizzly," Link jibed.

"I'm not afraid of little ones. Of course, I suppose you prefer the big ones? Maybe that's why you're so calm? And you're sweating because it's so hot out here? Right?"

Link grinned and sat down. The first pale stars glittered in the sky, and the moon rose. Its light reflected in the river, turning it into a flowing, golden ribbon. Antray got up to walk restlessly to one end of the raft and back again.

"I don't think so much of your ideas, old chap. Right offhand I can imagine six hundred and thirteen places where I'd rather spend the night."

"Yeah. So can I, but one place I can think of that'd be worse than this is a tree. Ever try hanging onto a branch for eight or ten hours?"

"I've missed that pleasure."

"Continue to miss it," Link advised shortly. "At least you can move around here."

"Sorry, Link. It wasn't so very long ago that I advised you to keep your perspective and here I go losing mine. It won't happen again. I'll try to appreciate the comforts of home."

With darkness, the mountain cold came. It was a penetrating chill, and the shirts and trousers the two men wore provided small barrier to it. Frost sparkled in the air. Fortunately it was not windy; only a gentle breeze ruffled the tops of the forest trees. A weird cacophony of snarls and screeches rose as two creatures, meeting, battled for the right of way. Listening attentively, Link decided that a prowling wolf had met a lynx on the ground. The sounds of battle died.

Link shivered, and beat his hands together to warm them. Though they were not going to freeze, they were going to be very cold, and sleep for either man would be out of the question. At least the moon was up; its light would be a comfort, and show the passage of time.

Link fretted inwardly. Time never passed more slowly than it did when he was confined in a small place and could do nothing about it. It seemed that the night should be half gone, but probably they had been on the raft less than an hour. Link looked at the peaks, so dimly outlined against the sky that they looked like massed cloud formations. Somewhere out there Garridge huddled near his lonely fire, hopefully on his way toward what he thought was the pass.

There was a flash of wings against the sky as an owl flew up the river. It dipped toward the forest and disappeared, and there was a muffled squeak as it swooped to catch its prey. Antray watched speculatively.

"Wish the beggar would land here. I could eat him raw, feathers and all."

"We already have something raw to eat," Link

pointed out, "and the feathers have been removed."

"Is that an advantage?"

"I don't know. Do you want to find out?"

Antray shuddered. "Not yet. Civilized people don't do those things!"

Link stared down the moon-washed river, wishing there were some method by which he could exert mental will and quell the gnawing in his own stomach. Neither he nor Antray had eaten anything since early morning, and now the unseasoned grayling which Antray had broiled over an open fire seemed like the ultimate in delicacies. Link picked up and sniffed at the grouse. It looked, he thought, like a small dressed chicken and its smell was not unpleasant.

"How hungry are you?" he asked.

"Not that hungry. Hang it up. We'll find a way to start a fire and at least char the thing!"

"Will we?"

"Yes," Antray said flatly, as if he really believed it.

"Have a good whiff."

Link crossed the raft and held the dressed grouse beneath Antray's nose. The little man sniffed hungrily, then drew back and said accusingly, "You're trying to awaken the beast in me."

"It wouldn't be a bad idea. I suppose it has occurred to you that we are in a beast's land?"

"That it has. That it has."

There was a wild, shrill yell near the river's bank. Link looked toward it and he knew that Antray was looking, too. There was a moment's silence, then Antray spoke thoughtfully.

"Have you ever realized that, as a beast, man is rather indestructible?"

"I'm beginning to hope so."

"I mean it. Compared to any of the larger animals in the Caribous we're physical weaklings. Any wolf or bear could kill us. But they haven't."

"If we can help it, they won't."

"That's the point; we'll do our best to help it. Why do you think man not only survived but ruled, Link?"

"I wouldn't know."

"You must have some ideas. Twenty thousand years ago, or even less, all men were confronted with the same situation which you and I now face. Probably they had to battle beasts even more dangerous. The saber-toothed tiger undoubtedly made a shambles of many a village, or what passed for villages. Still, the saber-tooth is extinct and man lives. Why is it, Link?"

"I wouldn't have the least idea."

"Was it his superior intelligence, his adaptability to new situations, luck, or God? There has to be an answer. Some day I intend to find out!"

"You're in a good place to find out, right here,"

said Link grimly. "All you have to do is stay alive—and remember how you did it!"

"That's all there is to it, eh? All right, I'm going to eat. Give me some of your raw grouse!"

Link knelt on the raft, laid the dressed bird on one of the logs, and split it evenly with his jackknife. He weighed the two pieces in his hands, and gave half to Antray.

"Here. Just imagine it's roast turkey."

"Right-o."

Link bit into his section of the grouse. It was tough, stringy, and hard to bite. Man had indeed come a long way from the Stone Age, he reflected. Doubtless the ancient hunters used their teeth in battle when other weapons failed—and used them to good advantage. Probably their jaws were as strong as a wolf's. But cooked foods, civilized living, and lack of necessity for rending with the teeth had taken their inevitable toll of strength. It was hard to bite the grouse simply because his jaws and teeth were weak. Link ripped a bit of meat from the bird's leg and chewed it.

For a moment he was inclined to gag. Then the feeling of nausea passed as hunger triumphed. Raw grouse was not at all bad eating when nothing else was to be had. Link continued to eat, until he had gnawed the last shreds from the bones. The hunger ache in his belly lessened somewhat, but he was still hungry.

"How are you making it?" he asked Antray.

"All right, old chap. It isn't the gruesome business I'd thought it would be. Matter of fact, mine was downright tasty."

"Could you eat some more?"

"Rather a pointless question, isn't it, when there's no more to eat?"

"Just thought I'd ask."

Idly Link picked up one of the grouse's leg bones, twisting it around and around in his hands while he considered their situation. Nobody who went into the wilderness, and depended on the country for the larger part of his food, could be certain of getting anything to eat. Still, if there was any game at all, and the wilderness traveller understood hunting, sooner or later he would bag something. Always before Link had been equipped with the best of modern weapons. Now he had lost those weapons and had only his hands and brains to depend on. However, he had found within himself resources and crafts which he hadn't thought existed.

Link was unable to define the change exactly. He seemed closer to the wilderness, and suddenly able to understand its moods and ways as he never had before. He had a new sense of alertness and of intuition. Under ordinary circumstances he never would have thought of saving the grouse's head, feathers, and entrails, but some deep, warning voice had advised him not to throw them away.

Now, as he played with the bone, another idea was born.

He got up to walk around the raft, stamping his feet and beating his hands to warm himself. Then he sat down, took the jackknife from his pocket, and opened the smaller, broken blade. Carefully, for it would be near disaster to break the blade again, he sliced around and around the bone until he had cut the large knuckles from each end. Link whittled the two ends of the straight piece of bone that remained, working a sharp point on each.

Distant thunder rumbled, and a ragged streak of lightning ripped through the sky. Antray, weary to the point of exhaustion but too cold to sleep, huddled miserably in the center of the raft. Link did not look up. Carefully, not putting too much pressure on his knife blade, he worked a groove around the center of the pointed bone. Then he had an awl, sharp at both ends and with a groove worked around the center.

"What are you doing?" Antray asked.

"I," Link announced, "have become an inventor. Let me have that hank of fish line you were carrying in your pocket."

Antray got stiffly to his feet, teeth chattering, and thrust cold fingers into his pocket. He walked over to Link and handed him the fishing line. The little man's curiosity was evident as he bent close to the bone that Link held in his hand.

"Ingenious," he murmured. "What is it?"

"A Link Stevens Special, designed to revolutionize the fishing industry in the Caribous."

Link tied one end of the fish line around the groove he had cut in the bone, testing it carefully to make sure it was tight and that it would not slip to either side. Cutting a foot-long length from the other end of the line, he tied some of the grouse's entrails to the bone. Then he cast his baited bone into the river and let it float down.

Antray knelt beside him and for a few minutes both men forgot that they were cold and miserable. This was something new, exciting, something to take their minds from themselves. There was a savage strike and Link hauled in the stripped bone. He dangled it from his hand, and again the exciting tension of the hunt rose within him. Antray, beside him, seemed as tense. They were not fishing for sport or even for a variety in their food. A subtle difference had crept in. They were fishing because, if they did not get food of some sort, they would die.

"Pay out only half as much line," Antray suggested. "The next time you get a bite don't jerk at once. Let him swallow the bone with the bait, and then strike."

"That's what I'd hoped to do before, but it might be a good idea to let him run with some line."

Patiently Link tied another bit of waste to the bone and let it float down, but this time he kept half the line in his hand. There was a gentle tug, and Link let another six inches of line slip into the river. The tugging continued. Link gave more line, and more, and when he came almost to the end he jerked savagely.

The line tightened as the trout on the end made a wild lunge for freedom. Link played him gently, skillfully, unsure of how hard he was hooked. After ten minutes he brought a three-pound trout to the edge of the raft. Antray knelt to pass his fingers through the trout's gills and flip him up onto the raft. A wild jubilation coursed through Link. They had more food; they needn't starve.

"Let me try," Antray begged.

"Sure."

Link killed and dressed the trout, finding as he did so how well his improvised way of catching it had worked. The fish had swallowed the bone along with the bait, and when the line was jerked the bone had turned sideways. The fish could not possibly disgorge it and was hooked even more securely than he would have been on conventional tackle.

Antray baited, fished, and lost his bait. He lost another bait, but on the third try he landed a smaller trout. Link filleted both of them.

"How about some trout a la Caribou?"

"Fine; I can't wait."

Link ate, wondering as he did so why he had ever found eating uncooked food repugnant. They finished the two trout, and when they had eaten the last of them their hunger was satisfied.

"What time is it?" Antray inquired.

Link looked at the moon. "About midnight."

"And I could swear it's a week from next Tuesday," the little man said. "Have you ever been this cold before?"

"Not that I can remember."

Link thought of the many times he had bucked a hard trail with the temperature at forty or even fifty below. But he had been dressed for it, and exercising. He knew he would always remember this night spent on a raft moored in a wild and nameless river as the coldest of his life.

Antray tinkered with the fishing line, using the heads and entrails of the two trout for bait, and caught four more. Link walked around and around the raft, listening to the murmur of the river and to the various beasts that prowled the bank. He knew from the sounds that many stopped to look or smell, but none tried to get to the raft.

Another streak of lightning travelled raggedly across the sky, and thunder again muttered in the distance. A mountain storm was certainly in the making, but Link found himself not caring when it came. He and Antray could not be worse off than they already were. Pelting rain might even help them take their minds off present troubles.

The night was interminable, with every minute

an hour long and every hour a week. Link looked eagerly up when the sky seemed to lighten, and sank dejectedly back down. The night certainly had no ending.

But it did end at last. The overcast sky lightened, and grew pale with approaching dawn. Link stared at it, unable to believe that their vigil on the raft was over. But there was no doubt about it; he could make out the outlines of the trees.

"Antray!" he called sharply.

The little man was dozing, his head on his hunched knees.

"Uh . . . what?"

"It's morning."

Hand over hand, working together, they heaved the anchor from the bottom and laid it on the raft. Link pulled them in to shore, and bent down to pick up his lance and club. He tried to swing the club, and found that he could not; he was too stiff. Numb with cold and exposure, he turned to give Antray a hand. Painfully the little man clambered up beside him, and stood shivering while Link tied the raft securely to shore.

"Listen!" Antray said. "Something's coming."

Chiri bounded out of the trees.

9
The Cave

Chiri wagged up, rubbed his great head against Link's thigh and blissfully closed his eyes while his ears were scratched. But he flattened his ears and snarled at Antray when the little man came near. Link laid a quieting hand on Chiri's ruff and turned to Antray.

"Come on over. He must learn that we're travelling together, and I'm not going to let him out of my sight again. Chiri won't bother you as soon as he knows that I approve of you."

"Courage, Trigg," Antray muttered. "He looks rather wolfish to me. I hope you know what you're talking about."

"I do."

Antray walked up and stood beside Link. Link put a companionable hand on the little man's shoulder. For a moment Chiri held himself stiffly, then he walked indifferently away and pretended great interest in a clump of grass. Antray watched nervously.

"He didn't exactly overwhelm me with affection."

"He won't. But this puts a new face on the whole thing."

"How so?"

"We can travel now, get out of here. Do I have to point out that just hanging around the river doesn't offer a brilliant future? We've got to find Garridge. But in spite of these so-called lances and clubs, I doubt if we'd travel far on our own. Now we have a chance, as long as Chiri's with us. He's worth ten extra men in a situation like this."

Link had recovered all his old spirits and his willingness, with Chiri's help, to meet anything that came. He walked back to the raft, picked up Antray's four trout, and gave two of them to Chiri. As the big dog gobbled them Antray looked at Link in surprise.

"He's really the Prodigal Son, isn't he?"

"Not exactly. He can always get his own fatted calf. But if he's well fed he's more likely to stay with us. I hope he'll even hunt for us."

Antray looked skeptical. "That I want to see."

Chiri lifted his head, licked his chops, and wagged his tail at Link. Antray poked with his lance at a bug that crawled hurriedly along the ground and ducked beneath a leaf.

"What now, Dan'l Boone?" the little man demanded.

"We'll have to try to make it to the pass before Garridge does, and get the rifle back. Our chances of seeing civilization again will be about ten times as good as they are if we have it. There's a lot of country between the Caribous and home, and it's full of a lot of things that aren't going to like our looks."

Antray traced a little circle with the point of his lance. "It's a good idea, Link, but I'm not going."

"What are you talking about?"

"I've already told you that I doubt my ability to climb your blasted mountains at full gallop, or even at a slow walk. I'll make out here until you return for me."

"You're going with me!"

Antray shook his head. "Link, I'm not kidding myself. Not even a little bit. We need that rifle, and if we can handle him we need Garridge. Besides, we can't leave him here alone, in his condition. That adds up to only one answer. You have to go alone. I wish I could go, but I'll only slow you down."

"You won't be any handicap."

"Soft soap," Antray said, "is fine for washing your hands, but we don't need it here. You go ahead."

Link bit his lip. Obviously Antray meant what he said, but he couldn't stay here. If nothing else killed him, a few more nights on the raft would. Link cast about for an argument forceful enough to persuade him.

"I need your help."

"So-o," Antray smiled.

"I do. We're armed, if you'd call it that, with spears and clubs. Garridge has a rifle. Suppose he did let go of that rope, and purposely put out the fire, hoping we'd die? If we catch up with him he'll do his best to make sure the next time. It'll take both of us to get him. He isn't going to reach the pass immediately, and when he does it'll take him some little time to find the path. We'll take it easy. You can make it."

Antray looked at him steadily. "You wouldn't just say that?"

"I would not."

"Lead on."

Chiri sprang up to trot contentedly along when they cut inland from the river. Link travelled slowly, mindful of Antray's hurts, and Chiri frisked impatiently ahead. They stopped for a drink at one of the icy little streams that flowed into the river. Antray leaned on his lance, swinging his club with the other hand.

"Any ideas as to how we're going to get food?" he asked.

"Yeah."

"Suppose there are any trout in this stream?" Antray asked wistfully.

"How hungry are you?"

"Hungry enough to eat heads, bones, and fins."

"Hang on for a little while. We'll eat soon if my idea's a good one."

Link followed the little stream to a shallow place, waded across, and climbed the opposite bank. He turned to help Antray, but the little man refused his proffered hand, and scrambled up beside him. Chiri, coursing ahead, stopped to stand still and gaze steadily toward an opening that showed among the green trees. Link grew tense, and licked suddenly dry lips.

By himself Chiri was a peerless hunter, but Link had never tried to train him as a game dog. If Chiri would not hunt for them, he and Antray would be hard put to get sufficient food. Killing the spruce hen had been more than half luck, and there would be very few trout in the heights.

Link put a restraining hand on Chiri's neck and walked toward the clearing. He slowed down as he came near, and peered between the trees into the clearing. Near the far side, near the trees, a little herd of caribou cows and calves milled nervously. Chiri tensed himself. Link tightened his grip on the big dog's ruff.

"Can't let him go here," he whispered to Antray.

"Why not?"

"They're too close to the timber. They'll get into it before he can catch them, and then I don't know where he'll kill or when he'll come back. Can't risk it."

"You're the doctor."

Turning aside, Link walked on, toward the distant base of a mountain. Having scented game, keyed up to a hunt, Chiri remained tense. Link felt a mounting nervousness. Chiri had become almost their whole hope, and his plan had to work. They came upon two mule deer and again Link restrained the big dog.

Then, at the edge of a wide meadow, they surprised a grazing elk, a small bull that looked at them a second before turning to flee. Link released his hold on Chiri.

"Hi! Yi-yi! Take him!"

Chiri left his side, swift as a shot arrow, and leaped out after the elk. The bull began to run, laying his antlers back along his shoulders while he streaked across the meadow. But from the first it was a hopeless flight. A hundred and twenty yards from where he had started, Chiri overtook him and slashed at the big tendon in his rear leg. The elk faltered, turned, and tried to fight, supporting himself on three legs. Chiri circled him, awaiting an opportunity to strike again. He found it, and leaped at the bull's throat. When Link arrived, Chiri was standing triumphantly on his fallen quarry.

As Antray hobbled up, Chiri bristled, and showed his great teeth in a rippling snarl.

Crouching close to the ground, he began to stalk Antray. The little man halted and drew back.

"Chiri!" Link said sharply.

The dog halted and came back to Link, but continued to bristle while he looked intently at Antray. Chiri would share his kills with Link, but with no one else. Link understood that.

"Stay where you are," he called. "Don't try to come any nearer. I'll fix things."

"I haven't the least intention of coming nearer!" Antray assured him.

Link cut into the little bull, and threw Chiri a big chunk of the liver. Cutting another piece, he carried it over to Antray.

"Here. Try it."

"It looks downright inviting!"

"Sure does."

It seemed to Link that there was a long-ago yesterday when he would have shuddered at the very thought of eating any such thing raw. But yesterdays had no place in the Caribous. There was nothing except today, the only life there was, and whatever relaxed its vigilance or failed to eat today would be killed and eaten by something else tomorrow. Link ate his liver without a qualm.

Then, with his jackknife he set to work skinning the little bull. Expertly he sliced the skin away from one haunch and side, rolled the elk over, and skinned the other. Sinking his knife as deeply as it would go, he cut one haunch from the carcass and took the bone out of it. Link separated and boned the other haunch, and lay both on the fresh skin. Then he looked down at the polished antlers while another idea formed.

There was no telling how long he and Antray would be in the Caribous, when they would find Garridge, or even if they would find him. Meanwhile they would have to do the best they could with whatever they had. Their lances were now no more than pointed sticks. Link knew vaguely that ancient man had tipped his lances with stone, but he knew nothing whatever of stone chipping. Why wouldn't antler work as well? It was both resilient and tough, and though Link had never tried to work it he thought it could be done. He raised his club and smashed it as hard as he could down on the antlers. A wide strip of bark was ripped from the club, but the antler remained intact. Link raised his club to strike again, and at the same time he was warned by Chiri's growl.

Link whirled, snatching up his lance as he did so, and Chiri moved over to stand beside him. Two wolves, attracted by the scent of fresh meat, were coming purposefully toward him. Link set his lance, and called over his shoulder.

"Come here, Trigg!"

The wolves circled, heads bent and tails curled while they sought an opening. Both swung to look at the onrushing Antray, and then both slunk into the forest. The odds were too great; the wolves would seek other game.

Chiri swung on Antray and snarled warningly. A safe distance away, the little man stopped.

Link balanced his lance, half regretting that the wolves had not pressed their attack. Sooner or later he and Antray would have to meet a beast in combat, and only then would they know exactly how effective their weapons were. It would have been well to start with something no larger than a wolf.

Quieting the dog, Link again brought his club down on the antlers, and again, continuing until he had smashed off all the bigger tines. He thrust a foot-long spike with a sharp point into his belt and put the rest in his pockets. Then he folded the fresh elk hide over the two haunches of meat and shouldered his improvised pack.

Chiri paid little attention. The game was his, and to be defended by him, only so long as it lay where he had brought it down. After Link took charge, he also took the responsibility.

Link carried his pack to Antray.

"Grub and a blanket all at the same time," he announced.

"Do you mean we're going to sleep under that green hide?"

"Sure. It's one more blanket than we had last night. Have you forgotten that it was a bit chilly?"

"Not I. Lead on, cave man."

Link climbed steadily, setting a compass course to the place where Garridge would probably have gone if he followed the vague directions Link had given. The chances were good that he would devote some time to looking for the path up to the pass, it would not be easy to find. Almost certainly he would expect no pursuit, for as far as he knew both Link and Antray had been drowned in the river. It should be a simple matter to find the smoke from his fire.

Lightning flashed suddenly, and distant thunder growled. Strong wind ruffled the evergreen branches, and bent the slender tips of the trees all in one direction. The storm was coming, and soon. They came into straggling forest spotted with huge boulders and with smaller stones that had fallen down the slope. Farther up there was an uneven parapet along a granite cliff.

The wind whined louder, higher, and its touch was icy. The cloud banks were now angry black masses which were carried ever lower by the weight of the water they carried. Link waited for Antray.

"Can you hurry it a bit?"

Obviously weary, but climbing valiantly, Antray increased his hobbling walk to an awkward half-trot. The clouds had come far down the mountains now; the snow peaks were hidden. A flash of lightning revealed in stark outline a dead pine farther up the slope. Link fell back to give Antray a helping hand, and shouted at him above the rumble of the brewing storm.

"Somewhere among these boulders there must be some place we can crawl into and wait the storm out! I'm not anxious to get wet!"

"Nor I! I'm cold enough bone dry!"

They came to the parapet and swung left along it as the first cold drops of rain spilled out of the low-hanging clouds. The wind was increasing. Chiri, trotting ahead, stopped suddenly and bristled. Instinctively Link swung his lance up, ready to fight.

Antray pointed. "Look!"

Link saw a black hole looming in the face of the parapet. A musty animal odor floated out of the hole, and a well-defined path led away from it. Obviously some beast used the place as a lair. Link approached carefully.

Antray shuddered. "Gruesome place, what?"

"At least it's out of the rain."

Chiri dived into the hole and they heard him snuffling audibly about. A moment later he reappeared, his nose and head thrust out of the hole. The rain was falling harder and Chiri evidently had no intention of venturing into it.

"Nobody home," Link said. "In we go."

"Suppose the owner returns while we're here?"

"In this country possession is the law."

They had to stoop to enter the opening, but as

soon as they were inside they could stand erect. Dim light filtered into the cave, which was about twenty feet long by twelve wide. Animal smell was strong but not too unpleasant. Somewhere toward the back end of the cave water dripped. However, the floor was dry. The dripping water, which had probably hollowed the cave in the first place, must have its own subterranean outlet. Antray peered about.

"This is all right, what?"

"It's better than being out there."

The dripping rain mingled gently with the sound of the dripping water, so that it was difficult to tell which was inside and which out. Thunder muttered sullenly, then the storm broke with renewed fury. A bright flash of lightning illumined the entire inside of the cave.

"Link!" Antray cried excitedly, "Garridge has been here!"

"How do you know?"

"Wait for the next flash of lightning and look at the center of the floor. There's been a fire!"

In a moment there was another lightning flash, followed by thunder that seemed to jar the mountain. The lightning revealed Chiri stretched comfortably on the cave's floor, beside the unmistakable remains of a fire. Link waited a moment more, letting his eyes adjust themselves to the cave's gloomy light, then he walked up and knelt beside the fire-

place. There were a few bits of charred wood, dry
and hard, but no ashes and not the slightest smell of
fire. Garridge had not been here. Whoever
crouched over that fire had not done so recently.

There was another lightning flash and Link's eyes
were attracted to something on the wall. Briefly he
saw two crude drawings of animals, traced in some
reddish-brown pigment on the gray wall. Link stood
erect, gasping.

"What's that?" His whispered exclamation
echoed back from the walls of the cave.

"Something wrong?" Antray asked anxiously.

"Wait for the next flash of lightning and look at
the wall to your left."

Bright lightning followed a heavy blast of thunder, and Antray's sharp intake of breath betrayed
his own amazement.

Then blinding lightning was followed immediately by a roaring, exploding clap of thunder, and the
air was filled with the smell of ozone. For a brief
moment they both stood stunned. Then, without a
word or a backward glance, Link rushed into the
furious storm. There might be something out there,
something which he and Antray needed desperately. Link stood on the parapet and looked all around.
Then he saw what he had hoped to see.

Lightning, striking the dead pine, had split it
down the full length. Blue smoke curled from it,
and in spite of the downpour the dead tree was

already on fire. Link rushed toward it, knowing he had only a few minutes before rain would extinguish the flames.

10

Invader

After Link and Chiri had gone, Trigg Antray sank down on the floor of the cave, completely worn out. He had given his best, and though he never would have admitted it to Link, he hadn't any more to give. The climb to the cave had been nothing less than torture.

This was the end and Antray knew it. Somehow it seemed a fitting end for a rainbow-chaser such as he had been. All his life he had pursued will-o'-the-wisps, shadows which meant nothing to most people, but because he had shown great numbers of people that there was a life outside their own he had made a good enough living. Only, somehow, it was not enough. Somewhere along the line something had escaped him. Well, it was too late to find what it was. Now this cave, the home of a man of a hundred, or a thousand, or maybe ten or thirty thousand years ago, was a fitting place to be. He had always felt that there were many links between the past and the present, and he did not at all mind going back into the past.

Antray thought of Link Stevens, and smiled. From the first moment he had liked this wandering trapper who had appeared in a place which, Antray had been sure, no man on foot could reach. Link had given new life to a lagging hope, but even he was not a miracle worker. Antray sniffed at the electrified air. It was evident that lightning had struck something nearby, and Link had probably rushed out in the hope of getting fire from it, even though he should have known before he started that his chances of success were not one in a hundred.

Antray felt a pleasant lassitude. He was not now and never had been afraid. Even when he knew the plane was going to crash he had not known fear. All his life he had taken chances, depending on his own intelligence to get him out of places which most men never would have gone into. It was to be expected that, some time, he would not get out.

He looked once toward the rain-veiled opening of the cave and closed his eyes. Maybe he could sleep a little while; certainly he needed sleep. Then he heard movement and opened his eyes again. A shadow darkened the cave's dimly seen mouth. But there was no glow of fire with the shadow; Link had failed.

"No luck, eh?" he said dully.

There was no answer, but something scraped on

the pebbles at the entrance. Antray felt an uncon-
scious prickle at the back of his neck. Fighting to
remain calm, he quietly picked up his club and
lance and backed to the far end of the cave. Water,
trickling down from the roof, sent a clammy spray
into the air. Antray moved away from it.

"Link?" he said cautiously.

Again there was no answer. Antray bit his lips and
forced himself to keep still. Link had not answered,
therefore something else was coming in. What
could it be?

Antray gripped his lance in one hand, his club in
the other, and faced the cave's opening. Lightning
flashed, and for a horrible fleeting second he
thought he was looking at a man dressed in furry
skins—the original occupant of the cave. Then he
realized what it was.

It was a monster bear, a great grizzly whose rain-
wet fur was plastered tightly against its huge frame.
The cave was its home.

Trigg Antray stood perfectly still, balancing his
lance. This was not the first time he had faced such a
bear. But before he had had a rifle capable of killing
even a grizzly, or at least a means of escape from it.
Now he had neither. But nobody could read a bear's
mind or tell in advance what it would do. If Antray
stood still, perhaps the grizzly would merely snuffle
about, then turn around and leave the cave.

A soaked, stinking thing whose odor was that of a

rain-wet dog, the grizzly came all the way into the cave. It stopped, and it seemed to Antray in the semidarkness that it swung toward him. A snarling grunt came from the grizzly's lips; a trespasser had dared to enter its home lair.

Still fighting to remain calm, Trigg Antray tried to plan his own defense. He had helped skin a couple of grizzlies, and he knew that they had hides tough as iron. Beneath the hide were layers of fat and muscle. The great bears were literally armored tanks of the wilderness, and he could scarcely even hope to thrust a lance very far into this one with the strength of his arms alone. There had to be a better way.

Antray placed the butt of his lance against the cave's stone wall, holding its slim length firmly in his left hand and pointed at the dim bulk of the bear. The grizzly would come swiftly if it came. Let it impale itself by its own momentum. That mountain of flesh had more strength and impetus than twenty men. He grasped his club desperately in his right hand, and waited.

The grizzly launched its charge.

Backed against the stone wall, supporting his lance, Antray met it squarely. He felt the pointed spear pierce the bear's chest and slide in. Stopping suddenly, the grizzly wrenched the spear out of Antray's hands.

Roaring with pain and rage, it retreated to the

other side of the cave and slapped at the imbedded lance with one front paw. The green wood slid out of the bear's wounded chest, and the grizzly pounced upon it and rended it with teeth and claws.

Antray shivered in his corner of the cave, watching with fascinated eyes. The bear was all beast, wild and rage-consumed, and as such wasted its physical superiority. Even the slowest-thinking man would have thought to look for his real enemy. He would not have spent time on a spear that could never hurt him unless it were launched by another man's hands. But there was cold comfort for Antray in this realization. He could not escape, and when it had finished splintering the lance, the grizzly would renew its attack on him.

The club in his hands, Antray braced himself against the wall and waited. He swung the club a couple of times, to limber stiffened muscles.

Then, suddenly, the bear was no longer there. One second it had been within a few feet of him, roaring and slashing a threat of imminent death. The next it was a craven, timid beast that skulked across the opposite side of the cave and hurriedly loped out into the rain. Dazed, Antray became aware of the flaming torch, a magic wall of fire, that had come between himself and the grizzly. He saw Link Stevens holding that torch, he heard Chiri growling at the departed bear, he realized that his life had been saved by the miracle of fire. Terribly shaken, he sank down on the floor of the cave.

"Whew!" Link exclaimed. "That was close! When did *he* come?"

"A few minutes after you left." Antray gasped, staring at the flickering torch. "Quick!" he added with pathetic eagerness. "Let's have a fire!"

Link put down the slabs of wood with which he had shielded his torch from the rain, and held the blaze to them. The wet wood hissed and sputtered, but the pineknot torch continued to burn. And then the wood caught. A tongue of blue flame licked up, blue smoke curled away. Link and Antray watched, fascinated by a commonplace which both had seen so many times that they had given it scarcely a second thought. But they also knew what it meant to be without fire, and were overawed by the re-creation of the miracle.

The firelight dazzled Antray's eyes, but above and beyond that it gave him a deep inner warmth, a glow of faith and courage. It did not seem possible that, only a few short minutes ago, everything had been so utterly hopeless.

"Man's conquest of fire," he said slowly, "must have had a great deal to do with his survival."

"I wouldn't be surprised," said Link dryly.

"Just think. If man had not conquered fire, now there might not be any men. It's one of the things we take for granted, something our hairy ancestors did, so it isn't important any more. I doubt if any one thing *is* more important. Yes, we survived without fire but we wouldn't have if we hadn't planned for it and if we hadn't had your dog. But look at the great forward jump we've taken now that we have fire again! An hour ago we were shivering savages; now we're civilized men! Lacking fire, you never could have repelled that ugly brute! Has it occurred to you that if the bear, for instance, had put fire to his own uses back in the dim past, instead of man, bears probably would rule the world today!"

"You get the darndest ideas!" Link was adding the charred embers around the fireplace to his fire, and blowing them into life. "Would you mind coming out of the clouds long enough to keep this going while I rustle some more wood."

"It will be a privilege!"

Chiri kept beside him when Link walked back into the storm. Antray, still entranced, knelt beside the fire and blew gently on the glowing embers. He smiled warmly as the flames leaped higher. And he knew that, regardless of what the future might bring, never again would he see anything, or have anything, half as precious as this fire.

Link returned, dragging a big branch that had broken when the stub fell. He started snapping off the dead twigs and throwing them into the fire. Antray leaped erect.

"I'll get some more."

"You'd better let me do the hauling. How about

you breaking up some of these branches and feeding them to our fire?"

"Right-o!"

Antray went enthusiastically to work. Link made three more trips to the still-burning tree, and dragged a great supply of wood into the cave. Then he broke several sticks of green wood and stripped the twigs off. When he finally came back into the cave Antray had the fire leaping.

Its yellow glow revealed every detail of the cave's interior. The two painted animals stood out clearly, and seemed to leap and run as the fire alternately died a little, then flared higher. The damp back end of the cave glowed wetly; tiny trickles of water dribbled down it into some subterranean passage. At one side were two crumbling mounds of earth, evidently places which the cave's former occupants had used as beds or storage piles. There was no sign of any furs or blankets that might have covered the beds, but there was a heap of gnawed bones in one corner. Antray pawed curiously among them.

Link sliced four steaks from a haunch of elk and impaled them on green sticks which he braced against chunks of dead wood and leaned over the fire. He gave Chiri a big chunk of meat, and the masked-face dog lay down to hold it between his fore paws while he bit off great pieces. Link watched the cooking meat sputter over the fire.

Antray stopped his scraping in the heap of refuse

and straightened up. He gave a startled exclamation.

"Ah! The tools of our forefathers' trade!"

He came over to the fire carrying several bits of chipped stone in his hands. There were small arrowheads, a larger spear tip, and a still larger piece that must have been intended as a knife. Link examined them intently. They had been fashioned from flint-like rock of a type which he had not yet found in the Caribous, but there were extensive beds of such stone on the Gander. If the man, or men, whose cave they now occupied had travelled from the Gander to the Caribous, facing all the dangers they must have faced, and armed only with stone-tipped weapons, they had indeed been daring men. Link looked up from the ancient tools.

"What do you think they are?" he asked.

Antray shook an excited head. "I wouldn't know. I've studied the crafts of most North American Indians, and these are unlike anything I've ever seen."

"Who made them?"

"I plead ignorance. Perhaps a tribe of Indians. Possibly they were chipped by a race of men about whom we know nothing. Only careful study by experts can determine exactly what they are."

"Somebody will know."

"My dear boy, if you'll forgive me, you reflect the smugness of modern man who thinks that the book of knowledge has been read to the last page. Actually, the first page has scarcely been interpreted. I don't know what these things are. Perhaps they are a commonplace. Maybe they'll provide a clue to some of the few billion things which we have not yet discovered."

"Could be you're right. I know I've never seen anything like them. But suppose we eat now?"

"I've just been waiting for the word."

Carefully Antray put the artifacts in a corner and sat down by the fire. He picked up a steak, bit off a chunk, and chewed heartily. Link greedily attacked another. All winter long he had lived on meat and had considered it hardship. Never, he thought, had he eaten anything as delicious as the dried fruit brought in by John Murdock. But this charred, unseasoned elk steak was better. No matter what happened from now on, Link decided, he would not complain about it. Regardless of how bad things seemed, they could always be worse.

Antray wiped his greasy hands on an unburned piece of wood, and sighed blissfully.

"Ah! All the comforts of home once more. We have a fire, hot food, a nice elk-skin blanket—you know, of course, that not even millionaires sleep under fresh elk skins?"

Link grinned. "That's right."

"And you!" Antray added. "Your ability to tell a

convincing lie is not the least part of your charm, Link. When we had to eat raw fish and meat, you said it was delicious."

"Might as well."

"Right again. Well, what do you consider the proper course from here on?"

"I thought the idea was to find Garridge."

"You say that as though you were going to look for a lost dog in your own back yard. Have you forgotten that some of these wonderful little beasties might not like our tramping around? I can tell you from experience that standing off a grizzly with a lance such as we have is no fun. What are we going to do if we run across another grizzly that doesn't like our looks? What we need is a weapon with a longer range."

"Just what would you suggest?"

"I was thinking of a bow and arrow."

Link considered. "I had the same idea, and I know the bow's a good weapon. I think modern archers have killed almost every species of big game, including lions and grizzlies, with it. But they were experts and I've never shot a bow in my life, though I'm going to learn. Besides, a good bow is a precision instrument, and I doubt if we could make anything except a crude weapon with the tools we have. I don't think it would be effective even if we knew how to shoot it."

"I try to keep an open mind. Let's have your ideas."

Link frowned. "We can't hope to make or find any weapon that's much good. But we're not going to starve because Chiri will bring down all the meat we can possibly use. And we have fire, though darned if I've figured out a way to carry it with us."

Antray nodded. "Seems to me I've heard about torches, and carrying live coals buried in ashes."

"Yeah. I've heard the same things, but what have we got that we can carry live coals in? And I doubt if any torch will burn more than an hour or so at the most. Then we'll have to stop and kindle another fire so we can light another torch. That'll cut seriously into our time."

"We have to try something."

"All right, we'll take a torch and leave the fire banked. Then, if something goes wrong, we'll at least be able to get back to the cave. We'll have to watch ourselves, too. The jackknife's worth its weight in diamonds, though unless it's very important we must use it for nothing except to skin and cut up game. The knife isn't much good as a weapon, anyway; the blade isn't long enough. As you say, we need better weapons. I don't know how to improve a club, but I think we can improve our lances considerably. Then the idea is to find Garridge. We'll have a rifle as soon as we find him, always providing that we can take it away from him."

Antray laughed. "Simple little problems, eh? Proceed, master-mind. I presume that you have some idea as to how our lances should be improved? And while we're on the subject, I need another one. That blasted bear made toothpicks of mine."

"I'll get you one. Let's have that stone knife."

Night was gathering when Link went out of the cave to a dense growth of spruces. He selected and bent a slender sapling, and hacked at it with the edge of the stone knife. It was a crude and blunt instrument, a clumsy thing not worth a jackknife in any boy's pocket, but it did bite into the wood. Also, every time Link bore down, it bit into his hand. But the jackknife had to be saved for cutting up food. It would be little short of disastrous to break the blade.

Link massaged his bruised hand against his thigh. The knife had no proper edge, only sharp corners. It was almost impossible to whittle or slice with it, but after half an hour he felled the tree. Link dragged it into the cave, hacked the branches from it, smoothed the roughest places with the small blade of his jackknife, and then took the broken elk antlers from the pack.

He used the sharp point of one antler to drill a hole in the bigger end of the stick. It was slow and tedious work, pecking out a sliver of wood, discarding it, and pecking out another sliver. Antray, watching with interest, picked up the other wooden lance and began to work a hole in its end.

Link turned his bit of antler around, and tried to fit the large end into the hole. He could not. Patiently he set to work enlarging the hole, and tried again to fit the antler into it. On the third try he succeeded, and looked critically at the point he had fitted.

It was not going to work, he saw. More than half the four-inch antler fitted snugly into the hole, but it would pull out the first time he thrust it into anything and in time it would work loose even if he didn't thrust. It must be bound in some fashion and with something strong enough to hold it. Again using the small blade of his knife, Link split the end of the stick to the bottom of the hole he had made. He split it again, and whittled a small bit of wood from each side. Now the hole had two quarter-inch slots opposite each other and as deep as the hole. Link set the length of antler in place and pressed the ends of the stick down. He nodded approvingly.

The bit of antler was wider at the bottom than at the pointed top, and the ends of the stick folded around it. With the edge of the stone knife Link scraped the end of the pole to a sloping point that blended smoothly with the antler. Then he turned to Antray.

"Let's have the fish line."

Link bound the fish line around and around the end of his pole. He tied it, and tried to pull the antler loose. It was solidly imbedded; he could not budge it. In a similar fashion he put an antler point on the other lance, and then looked critically at both. They were infinitely better than they had been, but they were not good. Antray, however, was delighted. He picked up his lance and made a grand flourish with it.

"Now I'm ready for the worst!" he chortled. "Bring it on!"

Link grinned as he looked around the cave. On one side Chiri was scratching enthusiastically at a crevice in which a mouse lay hidden. There was a startled squeak, a patter of feet, and Chiri flung his hundred and forty pounds at the fleeing mouse. It feinted, escaped, and left him scratching foolishly at another crevice. Antray stopped making passes with his lance and watched.

"I'm acquiring more and more ideas for my thesis," he observed.

"What kind of ideas?"

"About the survival of man, of course. Your dog, able to kill wolves, spends his time chasing mice. Futile effort. Man himself has been guilty of futile effort, but he has a purpose beyond just existing. You know, of course, that we really have no right to be alive? There were at least a hundred hungry things that could have killed us, but they didn't because we outwitted them."

"Go on," Link said. "I don't suppose I could shut you up anyway."

"Ah! An eager audience! Well, I no longer think man ever was a beast. Ancient man might have had more hair than we, and a receding forehead and a sloping chin, but he was not an ape. From the very beginning he was a man. The spark was there, the light that distinguishes man from beast. He could think, he could reason."

"And he could talk!" Link grinned.

"Quite so. Being physically weak, man found out how to use a club, how to make a spear, and how to use a rock to bash in the brains of his enemies. Eventually he discovered the principle of the bow, the wheel, how to smelt iron, and all the rest. He is still going on. The greatest goals have not been reached."

"And what are they?"

"A better and higher destiny," Antray stated positively. "Wars and disasters, wherein a few thousand or a few million humans will be killed, may interrupt. But, in the face of history, they'll be minor affairs. Man has struggled mightily. He'll continue to struggle, and he will reach his goal. He—Link, are you yawning?"

"I'm tired."

"It is evident," Antray said, "that you do not wish to listen to noble thoughts. Move over!"

Antray lay down beside Link and stretched his feet toward the fire.

"Ah!" he said. "Real luxury!"

11

Pursuit

When morning came the rain had stopped. Clouds still rolled around the mountain sides, and the air was damp and heavy. The temperature hovered near the freezing point.

Link rose, rubbing his eyes and yawning, as he looked down at the still sleeping Antray. Because the fire kept the cave warm enough so that there was no need for covers, they had spread the elk skin with the hair side out and slept on rather than under it. Chiri wagged over to have his ears scratched. Presently Antray yawned sleepily, turned over, then sat up and stretched.

"Guess I didn't hear the alarm," he grinned.

"I forgot to set it," Link retorted.

"What time do you suppose it is, anyway?"

"Summer daylight starts early in these parts. I reckon it's about half-past three."

"What a heathenish time to get up!"

"Isn't it? But remember that we're men with a

purpose; we have to catch Garridge. We need a rifle."

"Good old Link. Always thinking of work."

"Work and win," Link said. "But you can sleep a little while. I have to cook breakfast."

"Never let it be said that Trigg Antray slumbered while there was work to be done. Besides, if I'm not watching, you'll probably grab most of the grub for yourself."

"Don't be so suspicious, but I probably would."

Link picked up a long stick and poked in the ashes of the fire. He exposed glowing coals, added wood, and the fire soon blazed up. Link cut a piece of meat for Chiri, put two more elk steaks to broiling over the fire, and looked at a pine knot in one of the pieces of wood that lay on the floor. He nibbled his lip thoughtfully. All problems were easy to solve if you only knew how to solve them. In this cave they had the safety and comfort of fire. Yet they could not stay in the cave if they were going to find Garridge. How could they take fire with them?

Link turned the cooking meat, turned it again, then handed a steak to Antray. The little man squatted on the floor, holding his meat in both hands while he ate. Link grinned. The scene in this cave could not have been too different when the cave's original occupants lived there. If Link and Antray wore skins instead of clothing, they would easily pass for cave men. And Chiri, very close to things wild, might well have been the dog that accompanied the cave men.

He finished eating and picked up the piece of wood with the knot in it. With an antler point he pried off excess splinters of wood, until he had a rough torch, with the knot in the end.

Antray watched him intently.

"You're going to try it, eh?"

"We've got to try something."

Link heaped more wood on the fire, piling it irregularly so there were air spaces, and waited until it blazed high. Then he covered it with wood ashes. The flames died, but the fire would continue to smolder and burn for many hours to come. If they returned to the cave almost any time within twenty-four hours, and perhaps longer, there would be glowing embers to start another fire. With the end of the pine knot Link scraped away enough ashes so that a small flame rose, and lighted the knot.

The resinous wood burned fiercely. Link grasped the torch by its unlighted end and held it upright to slow the burning. That helped, but the wood was both seasoned and impregnated with pitch. It would not last an hour.

Meantime Antray had put the rest of their meat in the elk skin, which he threw over his shoulder. Taking their antler-tipped spears and clubs, they started out of the cave. Chiri, fed and disinclined to violent exercise, paced contentedly by their side.

Link turned east, toward the pass, and climbed steadily. Chiri bristled at something in the forest, and they stopped. A silver-tip grizzly, possibly the same bear which had attacked Antray, emerged from the pines and halted. For a moment he stood still, his immense head swinging from side to side as he studied them. Then he turned swiftly back into the forest.

Link sighed with relief. A grizzly was a formidable foe even when faced with an express rifle; only by the wildest of luck could they hope to kill one with spears and clubs. But it was neither them nor their puny weapons that the bear feared. It was the fire. Link glanced gratefully at the torch in his hand. Within itself it was a totally inadequate weapon, but the fear it aroused in creatures that did not understand it was a powerful defense. Even the mighty grizzly dared not pit himself against fire.

Half an hour after they left the cave, the torch had burned out the knot and fire was creeping down the stick toward Link's hand. He stopped beside a little creek that bounced down a steep incline, and pulled some dry twigs from beneath a bushy spruce. Link arranged them on the ground, ignited them with what was left of the torch, and built his fire up. Then he found another torch, a knotty branch from a dead tree, and broke it off. Link laid the branch down with one end slanting against a rock, and broke it again with his foot. He picked up a yard-long piece with a knot on one end and looked speculatively at it.

"At least the method works," Antray pointed out.

"Yes, but I doubt if we're much more than a mile from the cave. We'll never get anywhere at this rate."

"Nor would we get anywhere staying in the cave."

"There has to be some better way."

Link walked to the little stream and lowered the knot into it. He held it there while the streamlet foamed around it. Chiri came down to lap up a drink, while Antray, frankly puzzled, scratched his head.

"If I may be so bold as to say so, that isn't gasoline. It won't burn."

"I have the same idea."

Presently Link took his knot out of the stream to the fire, and held it in the flames. It sputtered and hissed, then finally caught and burned. But this time it did not burn so fiercely; Link had to point the lighted end at the ground and let the flame crawl up to keep it alight.

"Ingenious, what?" Antray applauded.

"Sure, sure." Link was pleased. "Stevens, Antray, and Chiri, Fire Experts. Anything cheerfully burned up. Bet this'll last more than a few minutes."

They continued to climb into the heights, but had

to progress slowly because of Antray. The little man said nothing and offered no complaints, but obviously his injuries were anything but trivial. Every foot he climbed he paid for with his pain, but he still climbed. Link stopped so he could rest.

He looked across the valley to see his falls spilling over the cliff. It was still early morning and the sun was not yet high enough to have any appreciable effect on the snow and glaciers in the heights, therefore the cataract was still only a trickle. Link turned to go on, suiting his pace to Antray's.

Farther up the slope a pair of denned wolves began to moan warningly. Link swerved. Probably the most powerful urge possessed by any wild creature was the impulse to defend its young. Even fire was no guarantee that these wolves would hesitate to attack if they thought the safety of their cubs was involved. It was best not to tempt fate too far, and Link was not sure that spears would be effective against wolves. He would not seek trouble; they had enough already.

For half an hour the torch smoldered. Then, drying itself in the fire which consumed it, it burned more swiftly. It was still more than an hour before Link had to stop and kindle a new fire from which he could light another torch. Antray looked on as he worked.

"How much do you think we gained this time?"

"I don't know, but we're getting into the heights."

"That you needn't tell me," Antray said wearily.

Link turned to look with concern at him. Antray was fighting gamely to go on and he could ask no more. Link said nothing as he swung about to resume the line of march. He had cut his own speed in half so Antray could keep up, and so far there had been no necessity for fast travelling. But what if it should suddenly become necessary?

Antray called ahead to him. "Do you feel that anything's unusual, Link?"

"What do you mean?"

"It's probably silly, but I've had the feeling all day that we're being watched. The hair on the back of my neck's been prickling. You know that's supposed to be a survival of the superior senses possessed by ancient man, and if it hadn't been for superior senses—"

"Yeah, I know. That's another reason why man survived when he should have died. Sure, we're being watched. There are plenty of things up here that think they should keep an eye on us."

"Including Tom Garridge?"

"Maybe, but I doubt it. I do know he should be around here if he's trying to reach the pass."

"How do you intend to prove whether he is or not?"

"Prod around until we find him or don't."

"And if we don't?"

"I'm not a magician, Antray. All I can do is read the sign as I see it and play hunches. Right now, to be entirely frank, I'm playing a hunch. And let's hope it's a good one."

Three times more, before noon, they stopped to build fires and re-kindle their torch. When the sun was directly overhead, at high noon, Link stopped again to broil some meat. He looked speculatively at a snow bank on the slope above them, then at their rapidly dwindling supply of food. There was a lot of meat in both haunches of an elk, but Chiri always had a prodigious appetite and Link and Antray, having no other food and working hard, were eating twice as much meat as they normally would. Sometime tomorrow Chiri would have to hunt again. Link reached out to ruffle the big dog's ears.

Antray stretched beside the fire, pillowing his head on his hands and staring at the sky. Link stole a glance at him, and turned to look nervously toward the pass. An anxious foreboding sat heavily upon him. Garridge should not be too far away, and he had a rifle. When the time came to move in on him they would have to move fast, and Antray could not do that. Link threw more wood on the fire, and turned the meat.

Antray yawned and sat up.

"I had the most glorious dream," he announced. "There I was, comfortable in a luxurious hotel, and I rang for room service. They brought me a bushel of assorted vegetables, and six loaves of bread with a pound of butter for each. Just as I sat down to eat, what happened? I heard you heaping wood on this blasted fire so we can eat more meat!"

"I suppose man lived to rule the world so you could make a pig of yourself in a hotel?" Link scoffed. "Maybe you'd rather not eat?"

"It isn't that bad, my friend. Try me and find out."

With a grin Link passed over one of the pieces of meat, and picked up the other for himself. Chiri stretched full length, keeping his head up and snuffling the winds. Once or twice the big dog started nervously as he caught some strange scent. He was becoming restless, but up to now had seemed willing to stay with them as long as he got plenty to eat and they kept on the move.

Then the wind changed so that it was blowing directly down the slope and Chiri rose. He turned half around, with his nose pointing toward the snow bank. His ruff bristled, his lips curled soundlessly. Link gulped the last of his meal and stared in the direction the big dog was looking.

"What is it?" Antray asked.

"I don't know."

"Has the dog scented something?"

"Yes, but there's nothing in sight. I'll look around. You stay here."

Link grasped his club and lance. With Chiri beside him, he advanced cautiously. There was nothing except open meadow between the snow bank and himself, and he could see nothing in the meadow. His lance and club ready, Link continued toward the snow bank. He kept his eyes on Chiri, whose head remained up. The dog evidently saw nothing, but was depending on his nose. Link reached the snow bank and looked down at a line of tracks—human tracks.

They were fresh, left within the past few hours, for no melting snow had softened them. Link got down on his hands and knees to examine the tracks closely, then rose to look toward the pass. He saw nothing, but certainly Garridge had passed this way, and recently. Link looked into the hazy distance. He could not see the twin spires because they had not yet climbed high enough, but if Garridge had climbed almost any crag he had very probably been able to see them. They were distinctive, a unique landmark. Nobody could possibly mistake them for anything else. And the tracks leading across the snow were uniformly straight; the man who left them was heading for some definite goal.

Link looked back toward the fire, where Antray

was watching him questioningly. He walked swiftly back.

"It's Garridge," he announced. "His tracks are in the snow."

"Then let's get on."

Link shook his head. "Do you think you can find your way back to the cave?"

"What?"

"He's travelling fast, and if I can I want to catch him before he gets over the pass. There are a thousand places to hide and a half dozen different ways to go once he's down the other side. I'll have to make tracks to catch him."

"Link, he's dangerous! I can't let a man armed with a make-shift club and lance go alone to catch a man armed with a rifle!"

"You can't keep up."

Antray sighed heavily. When he spoke again his voice was spiritless. "All right. What's the plan?"

"Go back to the cave. Carry the torch with you and light as many more as you need on the way. Take the elk skin and all the meat that's left. Here's the knife. Build up the fire and wait for me."

"What if—"

"I'll be there. You may have to eat skimpy rations for a day or so, but we'll make it up when I come."

"Aren't you going to carry a torch?"

"It'll slow me down too much. Don't worry. Chiri and I will get along all right."

"Right-o," Antray tried to force some cheer into his voice. "Good hunting."

Chiri walked contentedly beside him, and Link did not look back as he resumed his eastward journey toward the pass. He tried to forget the wistful, disappointed longing on Antray's face. The little man wished desperately to go on solely because he wanted to help. He did not want Link to face the insane Garridge unaided. Antray's body was small, but his willingness to fight against any odds was unsurpassed. A grizzly had no more courage.

Link quickened his step, still trying to obliterate the memory of Antray's face. It had to be this way and Antray was intelligent enough to understand it. Garridge was mentally unbalanced, but he was strong. It would take a stronger and faster man to catch him. Link mounted a boulder and stood a moment while he searched for a tell-tale plume of smoke.

There was none, which seemed strange. Garridge had no good reason to expect pursuit unless, as Antray suggested, he had seen them coming. But he was not building fires and evidently was not stopping. Could he have an inkling that someone was trailing him? Perhaps he had seen smoke from one of their fires.

Chiri stopped suddenly, and strained into the wind. His ruff bristled. Link took a tight grip on his lance and club, and instinctively glanced at a hump-backed boulder that arched itself out of the earth a few feet to one side. He moved toward it, reaching down to grasp Chiri's ruff and pulling the big dog with him as he did so. Link stood uncertainly behind the boulder, studying the terrain ahead of him and glancing down at Chiri from time to time. Unless every advantage was on his side, no man armed with only a club and spear could hope successfully to fight one armed with a rifle. Link had to be ready in advance, and if possible see Garridge before Garridge saw him.

A minute later two gray wolves emerged from a straggling stand of wind-twisted spruces and trotted diagonally across the meadow. The wind brought them Link's and Chiri's scent. They stopped, raised curious heads, then trotted a little way toward the pair. Chiri tensed, ready to do whatever the situation called for. But the wolves were merely curious, and after staring for a moment they swerved back to their original course.

Link watched them out of sight, and sighed with relief. Speed was essential, and even though he might win, a fight at this time would interfere with his pursuit of Garridge. If he became hurt, that could slow him seriously. Stealing occasional glances at Chiri, and studying the country ahead of him, Link walked across the meadow and into the trees from which the wolves had emerged. He felt safe there. The tree trunks grew close together, and in spite of the fact that they were storm-lashed for most of the year, the bottom foliage was thick and heavy. It was impossible to see for more than a few feet in any direction, and if Garridge was there he would have to be almost beside Link before he could shoot. Chiri gave no sign that anything unusual was among the trees.

Link emerged on the other side of the trees and looked sharply at a snow bank in the next meadow. He had no way of knowing exactly where Garridge would go, but presumably any man trying to reach the pass would take the most direct route to it. Link had proceeded on that assumption. Now, if he had guessed rightly, he should find Garridge's trail across the snow bank.

Link left the trees, walked to the snow, and tested it with his foot. It was hard and brittle stuff, subjected to so many repeated thawings and freezings that it had almost the consistency of ice. Still, Link's foot left a visible impression in it. Garridge was a heavy man; if he had crossed he must have left traces of his crossing. Link followed the snow line, looking for tracks. Seeing none, he reversed his direction. He still found nothing and a great uneasiness rose within him.

What had Garridge done? The logical way to the pass from where Link had seen the first tracks would lead directly across this snow field. Garridge was not logical; he was unbalanced. There was no telling what he would do or try to do. Link stood a moment, considering.

Chiri went forward to thrust his nose deeply into the snow and snuffle. Link watched him absently. A good work dog was an invaluable beast, and Chiri was the best possible trail animal. If a work dog could be trained to hunt properly he would be even more indispensable, and Link had high hopes that Chiri could be trained as a game dog. But the difficulty was that Chiri was interested in all tracks; probably he was now snuffling at the warm scent of a mouse. To discourage him might mean that he would not again be interested in hunting for Link. But time was precious now. Link walked to Chiri's side and lifted the big dog's head. Chiri retreated a step, moving suddenly so that Link's hand slipped into the snow.

About to withdraw it, he probed around instead, excitement leaping within him. The snow into which his hand had slipped was soft and yielding, unlike the hard crust around it. Garridge *had* crossed the snow, but he had covered his tracks and covered them carefully. Beyond any doubt he knew that he was being pursued! Link scratched Chiri's ears gratefully. The big dog was not a trained man hunter, but nothing escaped him. Even though it was accidental, he had shown Link the path taken by Garridge.

Link crossed the snow bank and broke into a swift

trot, with Chiri loping easily beside him. Garridge probably had looked around the high country and fumbled a bit before he found the way. But he had found it now; at any rate, he was heading directly toward the pass. If possible, Link had to get there before he did. It would be a great advantage to climb the ledge and meet Garridge coming up. That way he had a chance.

An hour later Link reached the high wall leading to the pass and his heart sank. Garridge had already gone up; his tracks were plain in the light snow that dusted the ledge. Link glanced at the top of the wall, and licked dry lips. The ledge offered no protection whatever. A man standing on top could shoot at will anyone coming up from the bottom. But there was no other way. Link started up the path, sweat standing on his forehead. He reached the top safely; Garridge had not waited.

There had been a change on the mountain top since Link had first travelled it. Much snow was gone. Boulders and piles of boulders that had been covered were now revealed, and water running over snow and ice had worn deep ditches. But the twin spires showed plainly in the distance. This was the right path.

Link still had one great advantage. The trail across the mountain top was treacherous. Garridge would have to feel his way, and probe and choose. Probably, at times, he would have to retrace his steps. Link already knew the trail, and he started out at a dead run.

An hour later he sighted Garridge in the distance. Link continued to run. Chiri, perhaps getting Garridge's scent, dropped back to run beside him. The twin spires were much nearer, but Garridge was no longer in sight.

A rifle blasted suddenly and a bullet sang close to Link's head. He threw himself behind a boulder, pulling Chiri with him as he fell.

Garridge had planned a cunning ambush. Link was trapped.

12
Antray Waits

Trigg Antray watched Link and Chiri until they were out of sight. Then he turned and started slowly back toward the cave. There was nobody except himself now to make decisions; he would have to do things as he thought best. Had he had his way he would have gone with Link. But had he done so, Garridge would almost certainly have escaped. That much was evident from their painfully slow progress.

Antray smiled faintly. Not until he himself faced a primitive world with almost nothing had he fully realized that, in coming as far as it had, the human race had done so only by dint of violent, ceaseless struggle. Now he knew what primitive man had done in winning his struggle for food, for shelter, for protection from his enemies.

Superior weapons could not be the only reason for man's survival. At the beginning, there were dozens of creatures whose defensive and offensive armament was far better than that possessed by any human being. There was a great deal more to it, and Antray thought he had another part of the answer now.

Maybe man had survived partly because, in a very literal sense, he had always been his brother's helper if not his keeper. There must have been a great many times when ancient hunters, finding no game and encountering all sorts of rough travel and violent weather, were tempted to give up. They had kept going because if they had conceded that everything was hopeless, the people who were depending on them to bring food or to perform some other vital function would have suffered with them. Unquestionable proof of that was present right now: Link was the hunter, and he was the guardian of the home fire.

The morning's climb had exhausted Antray and he did not feel like walking back to the cave. Had the decision been his own he would not have returned. To do so meant that he would have to make the climb to the pass all over again. But Link Stevens had asked him to go back and keep the fire going, and Antray knew that Link was right. If everything went wrong, Link would expect to find him, and a fire, at the cave. Antray was doing something he did not want to do because someone else depended upon him to do it. Therefore he would exert himself.

He set his own pace, a very slow one, and grasped his blazing torch by the very tip. The torch was burning out fast and he had to have another one very soon. Fire meant safety. He quickened his steps; just ahead was a little patch of trees.

Reaching the trees, Antray put his torch on the ground, hobbled over to break some dry twigs, and laid them on the torch. Fire crackled and blazed up. He broke larger branches, and added them to his fire so it would not go out. Now he must find another suitable torch to carry.

Antray penetrated the little grove of trees, looking for a dead tree, or a dead branch which he might break. He pushed deeper and deeper into the trees, and brought up short. A yellow birch, sheltered by the surrounding evergreens, had found a rooting in the grove and a fat old porcupine sat placidly on one of the lower branches. The porcupine grunted querulously at the unwelcome disturber of its solitude, but it did not offer to move.

Antray scratched a puzzled head. He had been in the wilderness many times, but until now he had always been accompanied by a competent guide who packed plenty of provisions. He understood the desperation of his present position, and the importance of having as much food as he could possibly get. Probably he should now kill the porcupine with his lance.

Only how did one go about skinning a porcupine? Link would know, but Link wasn't there. Porcupines were laden with quills, and though Antray had never been thrust with one, he had studied them under the microscope. They were needle sharp, the points studded with numerous little barbs. It was easy to understand why they could inflict a painful wound.

There was something else to consider. Although the elk meat was more than half eaten, there was all Antray wanted to carry. The remains of the elk and the skin, as far as he was concerned, were a heavy load. To add the porcupine would make too heavy a burden, and there was little sense in killing anything unless he was sure he could use it.

Antray left the porcupine and wandered on. There seemed to be no dead knots, so as an experiment he grasped and broke a live twig. It came reluctantly away from the parent branch, leaving a long sliver of supple bark dangling down. Antray looked at the bark with great interest, then grasped it in his fingers and worked it back and forth. The bark was tough, resilient stuff. Antray twisted it from the tree and put it in his pocket. Such a specimen was certainly worth further study.

He looked anxiously back toward his fire. He had heaped a plentiful supply of wood on it, but dry wood burned very fast and the fire could not reasonably be expected to last very long. Taking a different way back to it, Antray almost stumbled over a dead spruce lying on the ground.

There was a branch sticking out with a knot at the end. Antray placed his foot against the trunk, grasped the branch, and pulled. Pain distorted his face, but the branch snapped off. He wiped the sweat from his face, and stood still a moment to recover his spent breath. Then he made his way to the dying fire and lighted his torch. He felt proud of himself.

A delighted smile crossed his lips when he noticed that the torch burned slowly. This was a new, important discovery. The tree had been lying on the ground for so long that it had absorbed moisture in the form of dew, rain, and melting snow. It burned well, but not nearly as fast as any of the torches Link had carried. Hereafter, he must remember to take knots from fallen trees.

An hour later the torch was still alight, but when Antray saw another he stopped to get it. A few hundred yards farther on he picked up a second. That was something else he must tell Link. If they gathered torches wherever it was convenient, they would not have to waste time looking for one when they needed it.

Antray continued his slow way back toward the cave. He came to a point opposite the falls and looked across at them. His interest quickened.

Link had made no specific mention of the cataract, but Antray had noted this morning that Link had paused for a few seconds to study it, and he had looked in the same direction. This morning only a trickle of water had spilled down the face of the cliff, but now a torrent was rushing over the same place. Antray laid the elk skin in which the meat was packed, his spare torches, and his club and lance on the ground. Retaining only the burning torch, he climbed a small knoll where he could get a better view.

Of course the reason for the vast increase in the cataract's volume was obvious. When they passed this morning, frost had still locked the source of the water. Now the sun had thawed the frozen uplands and there was much more water to spill down the falls. As always Antray was interested in both cause and effect. Everything had to be put in its proper place. This strange phenomenon ought to have significance over and above what appeared on the surface, but try as he would, Antray could not place that significance. For the moment, at least, it escaped him. However, it was something else to think about.

He started back to the place where he had left his gear, and broke into a sudden run. Two fisher which had emerged from some hiding place while he studied the cataract were tearing at the pack. Antray tried to run faster, and shouted as he ran.

"Hey! Get out of there!"

The fisher left, but when they did each bore in its mouth one of the two sections of elk meat which Antray had left. As they undulated over the ground, lithe and fast, Antray slowed to a walk. He could not possibly catch them. If he tried he would only waste more of his already wasted strength. He cursed his carelessness for creating a new problem. Everything had been bad enough before, but it was much worse now, for he had no food at all.

Antray picked up the elk skin. It had merely been folded around the meat, the legs tied so that the skin could be slung over one shoulder. The raiding fisher had not been interested in the skin, but only in the meat it enclosed, and the skin was not injured. He smoothed it and again slung it over his shoulder. From now on he must remember not to leave anything of value unprotected.

He looked back over the route he had come. He knew where there was a porcupine. Porcupines were easy game; almost anybody could kill one. But it was a long way back, he was very tired, and there would still be the problem of skinning it after he killed it. He was much nearer the cave than he was the porcupine. It seemed wisest to go on. Antray lighted another torch and resumed his journey.

The sun was still three hours high when he reached the cave. Antray entered cautiously; the place was empty. He used a stick to scrape ashes from the banked fire. Flame licked through the wood, and cast a cheerful glow against the cave's gloomy walls. Antray went out, and found the dead tree from which Link had taken their fire. The heavy rain had finally extinguished the burning tree, but a great many splinters and broken branches still lay around it. Antray gathered as many as he could carry and took them into the cave. He returned for another load, and another, until he had a huge pile of wood stacked around his fire. Darkness began to fall.

With it came loneliness, a haunting and dismal desolation such as Antray had never felt before. Even in the camp beside the river, with no hope of rescue, Garridge had been with him. Later, on the raft, with a still more hopeless outlook, he had had Link. In the last two days he had even become attached to Link's half-wild dog. Now he had nothing whatever, and Antray shivered with the coldness that that knowledge brought. He was alone and friendless, a speck in the endless wilderness. He gritted his teeth.

"Snap out of it!" he advised himself. "Pull yourself together. Thoughts like these started Tom Garridge chasing butterflies."

But he could not banish the loneliness which beset him. This, by far, was the worst experience he had suffered. It seemed that anything was bearable as long as somebody or something was present to offer companionship. No man was really sufficient unto himself; this loneliness was far worse than the hunger that gnawed at his belly. Antray pulled his belt in, but he could not alleviate the gnawing in his mind as easily.

Impulsively he plunged his hand into his pocket. His fingers touched the strip of bark he had placed there, and he drew it out. By the fire's leaping light he fell to examining the bark.

It was still supple and tough, filled with the sap that gave it life and growth. Antray began pulling it apart. It split easily, he found, but the tough fibers were very hard to break. He made a knot in one and pulled it tight. When it still did not break, a tremor of excitement thrilled through him.

A man never knew what he could do until he tried, and at least he now had something to try. He needn't sit the whole night through while loneliness tortured him. A busy mind and busy hands were seldom miserable. Antray picked up the elk skin and studied it carefully. It was not a large skin, but if he were sparing and careful, there should be enough material to make a jacket.

Of course the skin should be cured, but how? He was aware that primitive peoples had various methods of tanning hides. Some Indians made a paste of the animal's brains and used that as a curing agent. He had read that Eskimo women kept their men's clothing pliable by chewing. Antray grimaced distastefully. A skin that was worn constantly should remain fairly soft anyway, and any sort of jacket would be better than none at all. The elk skin had proven itself of little use as either a mattress or a blanket. Its only practical value had been as an improvised knapsack, but now there was nothing to carry.

Antray held one of the skinned-out front legs against his arm, measured it, and cut it off with the small blade of Link's knife. He cut the other front leg exactly the same length and folded the two around his arm. A pleased smile flitted across his face. As far as he knew nobody else in the world had ever made a jacket as he intended to make his, but he knew of no other way and the idea seemed feasible. Laying the two strips of skin together, with the hair side in, he punched tiny holes at half-inch intervals.

He worked carefully, absorbed in what he was doing, and while he worked he forgot completely the fact that he was a puny human being lost in a gigantic ocean of wilderness. His was the restless mind of an intelligent man, and as long as his mind could be occupied he would know peace.

Antray laid his two strips of skin together and separated a fiber from the piece of bark. He threaded the bark through two opposite holes, bent it around, and tied it. Painstakingly he tied the next two, and the two after that. Then he became worried.

He had only a small strip of bark left and it would not last very long. Antray split the fibers ever more finely as he drew toward the end, but before he was finished he had no more. He picked up the half-sewn sleeve and dangled it from his hand. The bark fibers might dry and split, but for the present they held. And there was an endless supply of this sort of sewing material in the Caribous. Antray looked wistfully toward the mouth of the cave.

He would have liked to go out but he dared not while it was dark. He threw more wood on the fire and watched it blaze up. Again he turned his eyes toward the cave's opening. If he had more bark he could work on the jacket until sheer exhaustion put him to sleep. But getting more tonight was out of the question. Antray got up to walk restlessly around the fire. Then a happy thought brought him back to the elk skin.

He could not sew it, but at least he could cut the rest to size and get it ready to sew. Antray cut his other sleeve from the two rear legs. He looked at the remaining skin, then doubled it and cut a hole big enough for his head to go through. He draped it over himself, with the hair next to his body. It would do. Antray removed the elk skin and sat down near the fire, piercing it with holes to be tied together with bark fibers.

The night should be almost gone, but he knew that it was not. Time never passed so slowly as when one wished it to pass. Possibly six hours had elapsed since he reached the cave, therefore it still lacked an hour until midnight. Daylight, when he could move freely outside, would come again at half-past three. The hours that must pass until then seemed endless.

Antray heaped more wood on the fire, and gave himself over to an intense study of the different patterns cast by the dancing flames. Fire was a fascinating subject, and one that he must some day study completely . . .

Antray jerked his head and blinked his eyes. He looked at the smoldering fire, and at the gray daylight that outlined the mouth of the cave. Obviously he had been asleep. But now it was daylight and a new hope seized him.

The very fact that daylight had come was enough, for now he would not have to endure the endless night hours. He could be busy, get some more bark and finish his jacket. Perhaps, he thought, he would even make and set some rabbit snares. He knew how that was done, and he was very hungry. Throwing an armload of wood on the fire, he walked to the mouth of the cave and looked around.

He opened the small blade of Link's knife, went to a tree, and cut a branch. It was not going to work, he saw, for when he cut he sliced through the bark. Grasping a small branch, he jerked it off. That was better; a long strip of bark was left hanging. Antray rolled it up, put it into his pocket, and gathered more. He experimented with some of the smaller twigs, bending them in a complete circle and tying the ends. When he found that they were supple enough to permit a knot, he gathered more. Small twigs should work quite as well as the bark fibers.

Antray came to a thick cluster of trees with a small, well-defined trail threading through them. It was a snowshoe rabbit trace, one of the many paths the big-footed hares used to travel from one place to another. He took several strips of bark from his pocket, and knotted two together. They broke when he exerted only a slight tension; he had tied them wrong. Antray tried again, tying several strips with the same knot fishermen use to tie delicate gut leaders. Now the bark held.

Next he cut three small sticks, notching two and scraping the third down to angled ends. He thrust the notched sticks upright in the ground, placed the angled stick in the notches, made a loop in his string of bark, and wound it twice around the angled stick. He tied the other end of his snare to a bent limb. A rabbit, coming along this trace, would dislodge the cross stick with his back. When he did that the tree limb would spring back and tighten the noose. Antray set more snares and returned to the cave to wait.

For an hour he worked on his jacket, an inner excitement gripping him. He had never thought himself capable of meeting the wilderness on its own terms, unequipped with all the devices of civilization. But now he certainly had a fine opportunity to find out whether he could or not. After an hour he went out to look at his rabbit snares.

Nothing had bothered the first. Something had become entangled in the second and had torn the snare to pieces. The bark was not strong enough to withstand a struggle. The next three snares were undisturbed, but Antray did not lose hope as he approached the last one. He saw movement there, and ran forward eagerly.

A small snowshoe, wearing the summer brown of his tribe, had been caught. Apparently it had tripped the snare only a moment or two before. Antray gripped the trembling thing tightly enough so it could not escape, and held it close against him. Even now it made no attempt to escape, nor did it try to bite. Antray carried his prize back to the cave. Now he could eat.

Again in the cave, he held the rabbit with both hands and felt its heart beating against his palms.

Antray licked his lips. There was no mercy in the wilderness, and he was very hungry. He looked at the rabbit again, then around the cave.

A subtle change seemed to have crept in. He was no longer alone, and the demons that had plagued him last night seemed banished by the very fact that he had company. Of course it was only a rabbit, but it was a living thing—tangible proof that something besides himself existed in this lost world.

Antray jerked his head in irritation. He was being stupidly sentimental, he told himself. A man should have a coldly practical mind; no other kind ever did him any real good. But, Antray assured himself, a man should also take the long view. He was hungry now, but he'd be a lot hungrier soon. It was all right to save the rabbit for a while. He'd kill and eat it later.

Holding the rabbit with one hand, Antray built a cage of loose rocks. He placed the rabbit within, and closed the top with a slab of wood. It was a good, practical arrangement, he thought, one any outdoorsman might well be proud of. He was saving food for the future. Antray went out to pluck some green grass for the rabbit, and after a few tries the creature ate from his hand. It was surprising how quickly it lost its fear.

Antray re-set his rabbit snares; he'd caught one and surely he should be able to catch another. But he didn't. More of his snares were ripped to bits without holding anything. Antray worked on his jacket and thought about the rabbit. Tonight he would surely kill and eat it. Before darkness fell he carried a great pile of wood into the cave.

Night came and he looked again at the rabbit. He was hungry, hungrier than he had ever been before, it seemed, but he wasn't lonely. He'd save the rabbit. But if Link did not come by tomorrow noon, certainly he would kill and eat his captive.

But noon came and Link had not yet arrived.

13

The Pass

Link Stevens, crouching behind the boulder, passed an arm around Chiri's neck and drew the big dog a little closer to him. The shot had come from ahead, in the direction of the spires, and Chiri was exposed where he had been standing. Angry fire shone in Link's eyes, for now everything was plain.

From the very first, Garridge had meant to kill. When he had deserted Link and Antray beside the river, and taken everything, it was his hope that they would drown or die there. Why, only Garridge could explain. He must have known that Antray could climb only slowly. Perhaps he had long ago realized the hopelessness of trying to escape down the river, and he did not wish to be impeded by a cripple on an attempt to go through the pass. Possibly Garridge had conceived a hatred for Antray; this often happened when two men had no company save each other. Or maybe Garridge, in his madness, had merely reacted to what at the time had seemed a heaven-sent opportunity.

Link's anger softened. He was not dealing with a normal man, but with an insane person; he could not afford to forget that. Garridge needed sympathy, not censure. If it were at all possible he had to be captured and, if necessary, forced to go along with Link and Antray. There were doctors who knew how to treat such as he, but there was no hope for him until he was out of the Caribous.

None of this erased the fact that Garridge was a very dangerous man. He was insane, but he could lay an expert ambush and knew how to shoot the rifle he carried. A few inches to the right and his bullet would have caught Link squarely in the head. That was good shooting in anybody's language. Since Garridge knew how to shoot that well, probably he also knew how to compensate so his next bullet would go where he wished.

Link remained behind the boulder, raising his eyes just far enough so he could look over the top. After losing sight of Garridge he had not seen him again, nor even a flash of sunlight gleaming from the muzzle of his rifle. That, and the sound of the rifle, told him certain facts. Had Garridge been close, Link would have seen some motion. The shot had come from nearly three hundred yards away and perhaps farther. Within itself, that was a deadly warning. Garridge knew how to shoot.

Chiri tensed himself, and snuffled the winds that swirled around their hiding place. Link watched him carefully, but the big dog offered no positive reaction beyond the fact that he knew someone else was near. The wind had come up strongly behind them and was blowing straight toward the spires. Probably Chiri could no longer get Garridge's scent.

Link edged around the boulder. Garridge might be ready to shoot at either man or dog, and though Chiri knew well the power of a rifle he had never been hurt by a bullet. Possibly he would show himself and draw fire. Link worried. For the first time Chiri was a distinct handicap. The fact that Link not only had to get himself out of the trap into which he had fallen, but had to take Chiri with him, made it twice as difficult. Chiri never had liked being shoved around.

The big dog pulled restlessly away from Link and walked to the edge of the boulder. When Link snapped his fingers he looked inquiringly around and came back to stand beside his master. He sat down, bushy tail flat on the ground, while he waited expectantly. Link considered the next move.

Garridge could not have chosen a place more ideally suited for ambush. Thirty feet to one side was a nest of boulders that straggled across the barren mountain top, but aside from those the only shelter was the big boulder behind which Link crouched. He dared not move, for if he left the protection he had Garridge could shoot at will. There was no reason to suppose that he would miss a second time.

Finally, weary of inaction, Chiri walked out from behind the boulder. True to his training, he did not move openly, as a dog would, but slunk wolf-fashion. The gray earth was almost a match for his gray coat. Link watched, holding his breath and fearing to speak. A moving target was always more difficult than a stationary one, and Chiri was moving. If Link gave an order he might stop to find out what was wanted. For what seemed like hours Link awaited the shot which he feared would follow the dog's appearance.

It came, a rifle blast that rolled across the mountain and left echoes bounding back from windswept black crags that rose above the snow line. Chiri jumped convulsively, seemed to stand for a split second, then gave a great leap into the nest of boulders.

Almost before the sound of the rifle died away, Link was on his feet and running. Garridge's rifle, the one he had taken from Link, held five cartridges. After shooting once it would take Garridge some little time, perhaps a second and a half, to lever another cartridge into firing position and sight again. A man in a hurry could travel a goodly distance in that time.

Link threw himself down among the nest of boulders a split second before another bullet whined over his head. He had timed things right. What was more, he now had some freedom to move about. There were many boulders here and they were close together. Only if the wildest luck were on his side could even an expert rifleman hope to aim, shoot, and hit a man dodging from one to another. Link made his way to Chiri.

The big dog was tense now, thoroughly alert and thoroughly angry. Link searched him over, and found a spot of blood on his back. He parted Chiri's long hair to find a scratch on his back, a bullet burn. Garridge had aimed just a bit too high.

There was no doubt that Chiri knew the power of a rifle. When they were out, and Link shot, Chiri always came running to see what had been brought down. If he should connect the blast of a rifle with injury to himself, and in any way link that up with Garridge, then nothing could stop his tearing Garridge's throat out should the opportunity present.

Link hoped Chiri was not capable of such reasoning. Garridge was to be pitied, not hated. He was scarcely responsible for anything he did, and though he was using an expert's skill he was not thinking clearly. If he were it would have occurred to him that Link had no rifle, and that it would be the essence of simplicity to come and kill him. Link decided that he was afraid to come, that he was concerned only with escape. Maybe Garridge's twisted mind had led him into the belief that Link had a rifle.

On the second and third shots Link had located Garridge's hiding place. He lay among a pile of boulders perhaps three hundred yards down the trail, and there was no possibility of dislodging him at the present time. Link continued to crawl among the boulders until he was about two hundred yards from the place at which he had entered them. He did not believe Garridge had seen him go there, for he drew no fire, and once he had put sufficient distance between himself and the madman Link settled down to wait.

Now, at least for the moment, he had regained some slight advantage. Garridge no longer knew exactly where he was and any move on Link's part would necessarily be something of a surprise. Chiri crawled with him when Link moved, so he stopped worrying about the big dog. Bullet-burned once, Chiri did not need another lesson.

Link waited as only a hunter knows how to wait. It would be folly to attack Garridge in his present position, for Link had no possibility of doing so successfully. A man armed with a club and spear could not hope openly to fight one armed with a rifle.

As the sun began to go down, Link lifted his head

to study the terrain ahead of him. A little way
beyond was another cluster of boulders, and beyond
that a huge rock imbedded in a hillside. If he could
map out some reasonable route that ran parallel to
the trail, then he would not have to venture back
onto it.

In his mind's eye he mapped out such a path, but
he dared not move until night had fallen. Then,
rising, he ran swiftly but silently along the route he
had chosen. Link came to the rounded boulder that
marked the end of the distance he had been able to
see, and had to proceed more cautiously. He had
known what lay ahead of him this far, but had not
been able to see what was beyond. Running silently
beside him, Chiri slowed when Link did. They
crept on quietly.

The big dog came to a sliding halt. Link heard
pebbles rattle. A moment later they bounced from a
ledge far below, and after that they fell into the
bottom of a crevasse. Now Link had to feel his way
around the edge of the drop-off. It was slow and
nerve-racking work, but he had no other choice.
Link continued to advance, using the shaft of his
lance to probe ahead.

He was worried about his footing, but not about
the time element. Garridge had to find the trail,
and in the darkness certainly he could go no faster
than Link. If Link won his gamble, and was able to
cut in ahead, he would have gained a tremendous

advantage. Garridge must expect that he would come from behind.

Link crawled over a small glacier, again using the lance to steady himself on the slippery footing it offered. Once or twice he dropped his hand on Chiri's head, but the big dog's pads gripped the ice and he had no trouble. Safely across the glacier, Link veered back to the trail. Nearing it, he felt Chiri bristle, and slowed to a cautious walk. He reached the trail.

Garridge seemed to possess a cunning worthy of the wariest wolf. There was snow in the trail at this point, and feeling it, Link felt Garridge's footprints. He had out-guessed and out-travelled Link. Evidently he had crawled away from his hiding place while the sun was still up and gone down the trail. Chiri thrust his nose down to snuffle at the footprints. Link thought hard.

He had gambled and lost, and venturing off the trail at night was too dangerous a game to play again. He'd done it once, but there was no guarantee that he could do it a second time. He still hadn't lost everything. Garridge did not know the trail and he was now travelling it at night. He could not possibly travel fast without taking grave risks, and he must know that. There was still a chance of overtaking him. Besides, at night, he and Link were evenly matched. Nobody could shoot a rifle in the darkness and do it accurately.

For half an hour, with Chiri trotting quietly beside him, Link strode swiftly along. Then he stopped with a muffled exclamation.

The night had been almost inky black, but now the moon was rising. It came up over the black crags, full and round. Its pale light fell softly over everything, so that every boulder lay in dim outline. The darkness melted.

Link walked on. There was nothing to be gained by stopping and Garridge must be overtaken. The rifle was necessary if they hoped to get safely back to the Gander, and Link had not yet lost. The moonlight almost matched the light of day, but it was deceptive. It was not a shooting light. Nobody could use it to line up the sights of a rifle with even reasonable accuracy. Garridge's possession of the rifle would not give him back his great advantage until the sun rose.

Daylight came, but no moving figure was to be seen. Garridge was not only a strong traveller but a sure one. He must have crossed strange mountain tops before; at any rate he certainly knew how to get across this one. The sun appeared, but Link did not stop. There was nothing he could do except go on, depend on Chiri to warn him of another ambush, and hope the breaks would be in his favor when he met Garridge again. Link came to a long opening with no boulders in it and looked four hundred yards ahead to the next shelter.

He hesitated. This was another perfect place for an ambush. There was no way across the opening except straight ahead. Link looked down at Chiri. The big dog gave no sign that anyone might be lurking across the clearing, but a west wind still blew strongly. Even Chiri would have difficulty getting body scent at four hundred yards with the wind directly against him. Link decided to take a chance.

He was halfway across the clearing when he felt Chiri stiffen. A second later, holding the rifle with both hands, Garridge stepped out from behind a tall boulder.

Link halted where he was. Again he had blundered into a trap, but there had been no other way. Slowly, as though he knew that he had plenty of time and could not miss at such a distance, Garridge brought the rifle to his shoulder. Link fancied he heard the click when the safety was slipped.

"Don't shoot!" he called. "I'm your friend and I'll help you. I never tried to hurt you. Let me talk."

Garridge hesitated a bare second, then brought the rifle to his eye. Suddenly Link screamed.

"Watch out! Behind you!"

So stealthily had it come that Link barely made out the thing on top of the boulder which had sheltered Garridge. There were yellow colors on the bleak mountain top, and tawny hues, and browns. And what had settled on top of the boulder was all of them: it was a big cougar!

A second after Link screamed, the cougar detached itself from its lurking place. For a moment it was sharply etched against the sky, claws spread, tail straight out behind. Then, as it landed, the groping claws came together. There was a single muffled scream from Garridge and the rifle discharged harmlessly in the air.

For a shocked second, unable at once to grasp what had happened, Link remained rooted. Then he took a firm grip on his lance and club and ran forward. Chiri raced beside him.

The cougar's black-tipped ears were flat against its head. Its tail twitched angrily and its jaws parted in a snarl as it prepared to defend the prey which it had brought down. Chiri reached it first and the cougar's talon-tipped paws ripped at him. The big dog dodged the strike. The cougar turned its attention to Link.

The big cat crouched low on Garridge's body, lips still bared and tail twitching. A spitting snarl bubbled constantly in its throat. Straight at Link it launched its tawny, spring-steel length.

Link fought an impulse to run; he knew it would be fatal. The battle was joined and had to be fought to a finish. If he turned his back the cougar would spring upon him. Link levelled his lance.

Chiri flashed in from the side, striking with a wolfish slash at the cougar's undefended flank. At the same moment Link took two forward steps.

Muscles bulged as he thrust with all his strength. The antler-tipped spear pierced the cougar's chest, and punched its lethal way into vital organs. A flailing paw hooked Link's sleeve and ripped it to shreds.

The cougar writhed on the earth. He threw himself wildly about, tried to get up, then sank down and lay still.

Link knelt beside Garridge, but it was too late. Here on the barren mountain top the tortured man had finally found lasting peace. Link gently took the pack from his shoulders, then searched Garridge's pockets for whatever might be there. He took matches, a hunting knife, and all the cartridges Garridge had left. Lastly he stripped off his own jacket, which Garridge had been wearing, and tied it to the pack.

Link lifted Garridge's body to his shoulders and carried it into the cougar's den. He laid Garridge there, beside the bones of that other traveller who had dared try the mountain pass. Link stood for a moment with bowed head. He didn't know the proper prayers, but maybe The One who received Garridge next would know that a fellow man hoped he would be well received. Having done all he could, he left the cave.

Link examined the contents of the pack. His sleeping bag, cooking utensils, the axe, and a haunch of mountain sheep were still there. Link cut off a piece and gave it to Chiri, then shouldered the pack. Antray would be all right in the cave and he had enough food to see him through. Before he returned, Link decided, it would be well to scout through the pass. Perhaps enough snow had melted so that Antray would not have too difficult a time of it.

Link was a half mile from the twin spires when he saw the blockade. He stopped short, hoping his eyes had played him false. But they had not: while he was in the Caribous there had been a tremendous landslide. Tons of earth, rock, and ice had tumbled from the spires to close completely the narrow gap between them. For the first time Link was sick with hopelessness. He might climb that wall, but it would be very difficult.

Antray would never get up.

14

Return

Curled in his sleeping bag, with Chiri standing guard, Link camped that night on top of the mountain. Despite the lack of a fire, he felt safe. With the exception of mountain goats, very few animals of any sort visited these storm-blasted heights. If danger should threaten, Chiri would awaken him, and he had the rifle.

Link reached out in the darkness to feel the rifle's cool hardness. Antray had not yet got around to classifying firearms, and the part they had played in human progress, but probably he would think of that any day now. From Link's point of view, it must have been a large part. Again armed with a rifle, he could walk where he willed in the Caribous and fear nothing. The rifle made him superior to any beast.

Link thought about Antray, and smiled a little. Though inexperienced, the little man was practical and level-headed. He would get along all right.

Beyond any doubt he'd be waiting at the cave, with a dozen additional ideas as to why the human race had survived when by every law of averages it should have died. Maybe Antray had something, at that; he seemed determined to worry about the problem until he had found the whole solution. Link fell into a sound sleep.

He awakened with the first light of dawn, fed Chiri some of the mutton in his pack, and put the rest back with a grimace. Raw meat was a Godsend when you were very hungry and had nothing else, but he was not that hungry yet. In a few hours he would be down in the timber where he could have a fire. Carefully he unwrapped the fishing line from the end of his lance, put the line in his pocket and threw the lance aside. It had served him well, but he now had a better weapon.

As he started back down the trail, he looked once toward the spires. He had spent half the previous day in a vain search for a route Antray could travel. The pass was hopelessly closed. There was no use bewailing that fact, because there was nothing he could do about it. Still, there was no denying the seriousness of the predicament it left them in. Antray was badly in need of a doctor's attention.

With Chiri trotting beside him, Link walked down the ledge into the above-timberline meadows. He swerved to the forest, gathered and piled dry twigs, put a roll of feathery birch bark beneath them, and struck a match. He watched, raptly intent, as the match flared and then burned steadily. Link touched the match to the dry birch bark, and blew the match out after his fire was burning. For a long moment he stared at the charred match stick. Within itself a match was a miracle, and one to be doubly appreciated when one had desperate need of them. If Antray really intended to investigate the reasons for the human race as it was, he'd better start with fire.

Link cut and cooked a piece of mutton, and ate. He picked up his rifle, shouldered the pack, and continued toward the cave. He stopped in passing to look at the falls, now gushing a great volume, then went on. The outlet of the cataract still posed a question, and one to which he had not yet found an answer.

A quarter mile from the cave he stopped when he saw motion in the spruces. Link froze in his tracks, waiting to discover exactly what had moved. The motion was repeated; Link saw two buck deer walking almost side by side. He levelled his rifle, waited until one had drawn ahead of the other, sighted, and squeezed the trigger. The buck at which he had shot gave a great leap that carried him well into the spruces, stood for a moment while his head sank toward the ground, then slowly collapsed.

Link levered another cartridge into firing position and ran forward. They needed more food than he had in the pack, but he had purposely waited until he came nearer the cave so he would not have so far to carry it. Link skinned his buck, and took the haunches, loins, and liver. He wrapped them in the fresh hide and looked at the remaining meat. It was shameful to waste it, but there were times when the principles of sportsmanship must be sacrificed to the dictates of necessity. Link and Antray could neither carry nor use a whole buck—the meat would spoil—but not everything that remained had to be wasted. Link looked around for Chiri.

The big dog had been beside him only a few minutes ago, then had drifted away to snuffle at something. Now he was nowhere in sight. Link called.

"Chiri."

The dog did not appear and Link called again. When Chiri still failed to respond, Link shouldered his venison and resumed his journey. Probably Chiri had found something that interested him, and the chances were good that he would wander until he was tired. When he was ready he would come back. Link climbed the last little rise of ground to the cave and stopped in his tracks.

"What the blue blazes?"

Wearing his outlandish jacket, which covered him but bulged in back and at the sides, Trigg Antray was sitting in the sun in front of the cave. He was fondling a snowshoe rabbit that wriggled its nose and ate grass from his hand. Somehow Antray had contrived to comb his hair and had even trimmed a few straggling ends of his beard. The little man beamed happily.

"I heard you shoot. I trust you have brought something acceptable in the form of food? I'm starved."

Link remained dumbfounded. "Venison, but don't tell me you've run out of food."

Antray shook his head. "That's a long, dismal tale, Link. On my way back to the cave I foolishly allowed two four-footed robbers to steal my food. No, I have not eaten."

"You're sitting there with a rabbit in your hands."

"Not Peter, Link. Outwardly he may resemble a rabbit, but let me assure you that he is a most unusual beast. He's one of a long line of very distinguished animals. His family is adept at tearing bark snares to bits."

"You mean you made rabbit snares of bark, and actually caught something?"

"That I did, that I did. I caught Peter. He and I have had some long, refreshing conversations."

"They must have been pretty one-sided."

"Not at all. True, Peter lacks words, but he is most expressive in thumping the earth with his left hind foot. Or perhaps it's his right one, I forget. Why, eating Peter would be almost like eating my own brother."

"Now that you mention it there's a marked resemblance," Link grinned. "You both have long ears. I see you made yourself a jacket, too."

"There's a spark of jealousy in your eye," Antray said, "and I know it's because you didn't think of it first." Then his voice sobered. "What happened?"

"Garridge is dead."

The question in Antray's voice was reflected in his eyes. Link shook his head.

"No. I did not. I chased Garridge three-quarters of the way across the top of the mountain. A cougar got him."

Antray said, "I'm sorry."

"It was quick and easy, and maybe it was best. Garridge never knew what hit him."

"Poor old Tom," Antray murmured. "I'm still sorry."

"So am I."

Antray gently put his snowshoe rabbit on the ground. He looked up at Link.

"Where's Chiri?"

"Gone off to hunt."

"That's all I have to know."

Antray released the rabbit. For a moment it stood still, nose wrinkling and sides puffing. The rabbit hopped a little way and sat up. Then it bounded down the slope and disappeared among the spruces. Antray watched until his former captive was out of sight, then he smiled.

"There are times when a man's best friend is an animal."

"I believe you."

"I mean it, Link."

"And I still believe you. That's the way I feel about Chiri."

Antray eyed the bulging deer skin Link had brought. "There is too much chin-chopping going on around here. Let's eat."

"Not a bad idea."

Link entered the cave, impaled the buck's liver on a stick, and cooked it. He gave the largest part to Antray, and the little man ate hungrily. He wiped his hands on a bit of grass and sighed with satisfaction, licking his lips.

"That was worth waiting for. But what are you saving the rest for?"

"It'll be tough."

"My dear boy, I do not ask for gourmet's delight. All I want is something to eat."

Link sliced a steak from one of the haunches, and broiled that. Antray watched hungrily, fascinated by the sight of so much food, and when Link handed him the steak he ate as if he had had nothing before. He finished, sighed contentedly, and looked at Link.

"More?" Link asked.

"Thank you, no. But I am now prepared to face

anything. So give with the rest of the bad news."

"What?" Link was startled.

"Your face gives you away," Antray said quietly. "Let's have it."

Link blurted, "We aren't going through the pass."

"And why not?"

"Because we can't get through. It's been blocked by a landslide."

Antray looked at him steadily. "What now?"

Link glanced quickly at the little man. He had been almost afraid to tell Antray that they were hopelessly locked in the Caribous, but he should have known better. Antray had the courage to face anything.

"I was hoping you'd take it that way," Link said. "We aren't really so badly off. We have a rifle, axe, and hunting knife—and matches. Besides, there's Chiri. We won't starve. My idea is to go down into one of the valleys, perhaps back to the river, and build a good cabin. We can make things comfortable enough. After we're set for the winter we'll do all the exploring we can. There's sure to be another way out."

Antray said, "I think I'd like that."

"Good! Then let's do it."

"Whoa! Not so fast. I mean I'd like wintering here if I had my cameras, a few good books, and writing materials. Let's go back and get them first."

"What are you talking about?"

"Are you willing to take a chance?"

"Sure. What about it?"

"I sent a test raft down that river, and it got as far as the canyon safely. Then I lost sight of it."

"That may be, with a small, light raft. But look what happened when we tried to go down."

"Link, that test raft wasn't light. Garridge and I loaded it with boulders to make it heavier. The point is I launched my test raft in the afternoon, but we tried to go down in the morning."

"What's that got to do with it?"

"Have you noticed a falls, a cataract that spills about a thousand feet?"

"Sure, I've seen it several times," Link said impatiently. "Get to the point, will you?"

"When we saw that falls in the early morning only a little water was coming down it. When I came back that way later in the afternoon, it was a torrent. Every little ditch and drain was spilling water down the slope; every creek was swollen. Link, every afternoon that river receives a great additional volume of water. It's bound to have an effect. Possibly it will bring the river high enough so that, if we start in the afternoon, we can ride right over the rocks that tripped us last time."

"You're right!" Link cried excitedly.

"I *may* be right. At least we can go see."

Link looked admiringly at Antray. The little man

had thought of something which should have been perfectly obvious to him, but it hadn't been. It had taken applied reason to analyze the situation as Antray had done. Once it had been pointed out, anybody could see it.

Antray leaned back, and a sleeve split from his jacket.

"Blasted thing's always coming apart!" he complained.

Link grinned. "Bark isn't exactly the world's best thread. Take this jacket."

"I should say not!" Antray snorted. "You're just trying to get mine. I'll keep it, thank you."

"You won't keep it long unless you tie it better than that." Link reached into his pocket for the fish line he had taken from his spear. "Sew it with this."

"It's not primitive enough. Isn't there some of Mother Nature's material that will serve?"

"With all due respect to Mother Nature, she never made anything better than a processed fishing line. Use it."

"All right. But I do so under protest."

Patiently Antray strung the line through the holes he had punched in his jacket, and pulled experimentally at the seams. The fish line held, but Link hadn't had enough of it. Regretfully Antray looked at his lance, in which he took an enormous pride, then unwrapped the fish line that bound the point and finished his jacket. He put it on and posed.

"There! Ever see a better jacket?"

"I refuse to answer," Link grinned. "Probably it will keep you warm, if you can stand the smell. The sleeping bag will keep you even warmer, though. Go ahead and crawl into it."

"I'm not taking your sleeping bag."

"I say you are, and I can lick you."

"Violence is not admirable. I'll take it."

When morning came Chiri had not returned, but Link was unworried about him. Shouldering the pack and catching up the rifle, he led the way out of the cave and downhill. He struck a fast pace, ready to slow down should Antray show any signs of distress. But the little man seemed to have no trouble going downhill; only climbing bothered him. Link threaded his way among some windfall, slid down a steep slope, and came to level ground. He turned.

"You hungry?"

"I could eat."

"Seems to me you can always eat."

"One of my main talents," Antray admitted. "So get the fire going and the steaks on, chef. I'm really beginning to like the way you cook. When I give my next order in a restaurant, I'll have them take the meat back and burn it more so I can be reminded of the Caribous."

They built a fire and cooked venison. They ate, and went on. A half hour later Link stopped in his tracks.

He had seen motion among the trees, the barest flicker of something stirring in the brush. Link raised a cautioning hand, and slipped the rifle's safety catch. A second later the white moose broke cover.

It stood still, a freakish monster framed against green trees. Its head was up, its mane bristled, and leather lips rolled back from yellow tushes. The moose stamped an angry forefoot and tossed its head. Link lifted the rifle, but Antray struck the gun aside.

"That thing means business!" Link protested.

"Please don't shoot!" Antray gazed raptly at the moose. "Just look at him!"

"I'm looking! And he's looking at us!"

"What a rare beast," Antray murmured. "A very rare one. I wonder what his measurements are?"

"Just so he doesn't take ours. Watch out!"

The albino moose launched its charge. Three-quarters of a ton of fury, it trampled the brush and small trees in its path as it hurled itself straight at the two men. Antray scrambled for a tree, leaped to catch a low-hanging branch, and drew himself up. Link followed, and a split second after he was among the tree's branches a tip of one of the bull's antlers grazed his foot. The enraged moose whirled in half its own length and glared at them.

Clinging to a branch, his face alight with pleasure, Antray looked back. Link, thoroughly angry, fingered his rifle. He half-raised it to shoot, but brought it down again because of the sheer delight in Antray's words.

"Oh, for a camera! I never dreamed of having such an opportunity to see an albino moose at close range. What do you think of him, Link?"

"He's cute," Link sniffed.

Antray wasn't listening. "Do you think it could be a separate species of moose, Link? Or is he just a color phase, like an albino deer?"

"I wouldn't know, and to tell you the truth I don't much care. But you can depend on one thing; he's going to be a very dead moose if he doesn't get away from here in something less than two shakes of a lamb's tail."

"Oh no! He's worth real study!"

"You can study him even closer, and a lot safer, if I lay him out. But I'll hang off a while."

Antray never took his eyes from the white bull. The moose was pawing the earth with its front hoof now, and gave no sign of leaving. It came nearer the tree and looked up. Antray leaned down excitedly.

"I think his bone structure is exactly like that of a common moose! He's a color phase!"

"Wonderful. Learn one new thing each day."

"What a subject for a lecture!" Antray gloated. "Look at him, Link. He proves my theories all over again. If that bull had a man's brain he'd know that just bristling around would do him no good. He'd—"

The bull bumped the tree with his shoulder, and Antray grabbed wildly for a hand hold. Link wrapped both feet around the trunk and held on with one hand while he grasped the rifle with the other. The moose stepped back and the tree stopped quivering.

Link said, "Maybe he has his own ideas."

He had been treed by moose before, but never while he held a rifle in his hands. It would be so easy to get out of this, just one bullet would do it. Link glanced at Antray. Probably nobody else in the world would consider being treed by an angry bull moose a wonderful opportunity.

Then, after an hour, the bull drifted away. It went silently, incredibly softly for a thing of its bulk. Antray sighed.

"I told you he'd go."

"You sound disappointed about it."

"I'd like to have studied him more. I learned a lot."

"So did I, and one of the things I learned is to stay away from mad moose when you're with me."

"Well, we can get down now."

"Wait."

Link gave the rifle to Antray. "We'll take it a little easy. Maybe these brutes haven't got the brains of a man, but I've dealt with 'em before. Would you use the rifle if he cornered me?"

"Naturally."

"Get ready to use it, then."

Link dropped to the ground, just in time to get a springing start back into the tree. There was an angry grunt, the brush moved, and the bull moose charged out of it. Link settled beside Antray, who nodded his head.

"I understand!" he exclaimed. "He wanted us to think he'd gone away."

"You've hit it." Link's anger was rising again. "But with all due respect to you, and your playful little pet, I've sat in this tree about as long as I intend to. Give me the rifle."

"Don't shoot him!"

"I'm not going to. At least not right away."

Link waited until the moose had moved ten feet to one side, then aimed and pressed the trigger. The bullet skidded beneath the albino's belly, and kicked dirt and pine needles upward. The moose grunted angrily and began to paw the earth.

"He doesn't frighten easily," Antray observed.

"So I see."

The moose turned sideways, and looked in the direction from which Link and Antray had come.

Suddenly it turned and ran, disappearing like a white ghost among the trees. A moment later Chiri swept into view and ran past, following the bull's trail. Link and Antray heard him barking, and a moment later they heard water splashing as the albino bull entered an unseen lake or beaver dam. The two men swung out of the tree and flexed cramped muscles.

15

Escape

They reached Antray's old camp on the river bank at mid-morning. Outwardly there was little change; they hadn't been away long enough to permit any marked transformation. But the log shelter still seemed deserted and forlorn; it had the dismal air of a camp which has not been lived in. Antray grinned.

"Right back where we started from, eh? The Hotel Antray has guests once again."

"Yeah. Wonder if the plumbing is still working. Let's look at the river."

"A brilliant idea, my young friend."

Side by side they walked down to the river. It still surged swiftly between its banks, rippling where it poured over concealed rocks, foaming around exposed ones, calm nowhere. Link frowned. As far as he could see, the river had not changed in the slightest degree. But would any change be perceptible to the naked eye?

This was a wild river in every sense of the word.

The only bordering trees that had been disturbed were those few cut by Link, Antray, and Garridge. All rivers rose during the spring break-up, but after this one had received and carried off a great volume of melting snow and ice, certainly it would be subject to no flash floods. Trees and vegetation would absorb any heavy rain. If there was any day by day fluctuation in the river, it was very slight.

Antray asked, "What do you think?"

"Don't know what to think."

"Can it be that we're wrong? Does the river take the afternoon run-off with no effect whatever? Or does the run-off have some other outlet?"

"There's one way to find out."

Link caught up his axe and chopped a slender aspen. He cut a three-foot length and fashioned a point at one end. Then he used his hunting knife to cut a narrow circle of bark from the center of the stick, and took it down to the river. With the blunt end of his axe he pounded his stake in exactly at that point where water met land. He sank the stake to the mark he had made, and stepped back.

"Now all we have to do is watch it. If our guess was right, water should rise over that mark sometime this afternoon."

"Do you think we should keep a constant watch?"

"Since you suggested it, I think it would be a good idea if you did. You can devote your spare time to figuring out new reasons why the human race survived."

Link turned away from the river, continuing to hide beneath a mask of light-hearted humor the grave doubts and fears that assailed him. Despite the assurances he had given Antray, they had only the skimpiest of outfits for spending the winter anywhere in the wilderness. They could construct a warm cabin, but it would necessarily have to be a small and cramped one. With no saw for cutting wood, one man probably would have to spend all his time gathering firewood. They hadn't nearly enough matches to be on the safe side, and every remaining cartridge must account for a head of big game if they would have enough to eat. They had no snowshoes, but could contrive makeshift ones. They lacked completely all the little comforts that made winter life in the woods easier.

Besides, and most important, Antray had to see a doctor. He had been hurt, and only a skilled physician could cure whatever ailed him. Next spring might be too late. If there was even a faint chance of getting down the river, they had to take that chance now.

Chiri stayed beside him as Link cut wood, heaped some beside the log shelter, and built a fire up. He cut another aspen, imbedded it in the ground, braced it with sticks, and hung all the venison he had left over the fire. Once started down the river there would be no turning back, and Link wouldn't even venture a guess as to how long it would take them or what they would find. They had better think of everything, including cooked foods. It was entirely possible that they would have to spend a long while on the raft.

His camp chores finished, Link walked down to the river. Antray sat with his eyes on the marking stick, but his thoughts, as usual, were elsewhere.

"How goes the river?" Link called.

Antray waved a careless hand. "Flowing on in its ageless serenity. Caring not what happens to puny mortals. Surging steadily toward—"

"How's that again?"

"The river is not rising."

"Not at all?"

"Not one iota, unless your marker's moving with it."

Link knelt beside the stake. He squinted at it, then slowly rose. Antray was right. The river had not risen perceptibly; it was still level with the ring of bark he had peeled from the stick. Link looked up the river, and down it, as though the very intensity of his desire could bring on the hoped-for flood. Antray smiled.

"Not a very cooperative river, is it?" he said grimly.

"It doesn't seem to be. I suppose we might as well eat while we're waiting."

"An excellent idea. Lead on."

They ate their venison glumly, each trying hard to conceal his own uneasiness from the other. They had hoped the river would rise, for in the rise of water lay their only chance of getting over the rocks in the riffles. But it hadn't risen at all, and the sun was already directly overhead. The cataract would be hurling its torrents of water over the cliff. Unless the effect of that water showed on the river, they would not dare go down it. Link finished eating, and stretched out with his head pillowed on his hands. Chiri was sleeping in the sunshine. Antray glanced twice at the river, and idly traced designs on the ground with a stick he had picked up. He did not want to return to the marker, to read another discouraging message. But he kept his thoughts to himself.

"I've done the hard work all morning," he said. "Why don't you go look at the marker?"

Link made no move to get up and Antray looked narrowly at him. Obviously Link did not want to look at the marker either.

"I'll go myself, then," said Antray, "but some people around here sure are lazy."

He walked slowly down to the river and knelt beside the stick. His excited call floated back.

"Link! It's rising!"

"I'm coming!"

Link bounded up and ran down to the river. Antray's face shone with excitement.

"It's rising! Look for yourself!"

Link knelt beside the stick, and became almost as excited as Antray when he saw water a half inch over the mark on the stick; the river was definitely rising. Link stood up.

"We figured it wrong. The cataract and the other streams pick up as soon as the thaw in the heights sets in. It just takes time for everything to reach the river."

Now the water seemed to climb almost visibly around the stick, but there was still no change apparent in just a casual glance at the river itself. Link and Antray remained side by side, intent on the marker. In the middle of the afternoon the river reached its high level and stayed there. Link nicked the marker with his knife. Throughout the rest of the afternoon the water did not rise above the nick, but it stayed there. Twice after darkness set in, lighting his way with a burning brand, Link went down to re-examine their marker.

Shortly after dark the river began to fall, and two hours later it had lost more than half its afternoon gain. Link pulled the marker out and examined it. At its highest, the river had risen about two inches

above normal. Link returned to the blazing fire.
Antray made a dark silhouette on the near side, and
Chiri, returned from a rabbit hunt, lay full length
on the other. Link sat down and tried to analyze the
situation in the light of what they now knew.

They had already tried to go down the river, and
had come within a hair's breadth of disaster. If they
started in the middle of the afternoon, instead of in
the early morning, they would have two extra
inches of water. Was it enough of a safety margin? If
they had had that extra water before, would the raft
have ridden over the rocks? Link felt a sobering
doubt. On this attempt there would be nobody on
shore to help them out. Once launched they were
committed to the river trip. If they made it, what
lay in the canyon?

"Tomorrow we're on our way, Link," Antray said
cheerfully.

"Tomorrow it is." Link swallowed hard.

"Do you have any doubts about making it?"

"No."

Link clamped his jaw and tried to forget his
doubts. At the same time he knew that, if he were
alone, he would not take a chance on the river. Now
he had no choice. Trigg Antray had to get out of the
Caribous because if he did not it might be too late.
Link shrugged his shoulders, threw an armful of
wood on the fire, and watched a shower of sparks

float aloft. He lay down and slept peacefully. Now that he had committed himself to trying the river again, there was no sense in worrying about it.

Link woke very early, built up the fire, and for a while sat looking at the still sleeping Antray. The little man was an out and out theorist, but he had a hard core of practicality. Looking at the falls, he had decided that the river must rise after noon, which had not occurred to Link himself. But the details of the trip he had left to Link. Had he planned every-thing: food, equipment . . .? The raft! He had not gone to look at the raft yesterday! He had been so busy putting Antray's theories to a test that he had completely forgotten about the raft.

Link heated some of his already cooked meat, fed Chiri, and awakened Antray.

"Why such an early bird?"

"I want to take a look at the raft."

"We aren't leaving until mid-afternoon. The sun isn't even up yet."

"It'll be up soon enough."

Link led the way down-river. To his relief, he saw the raft where they had left it, in its mooring place. He looked critically at it. There was nothing wrong. Antray had made a good choice of materials; the raft rode high in the water.

Then he thought of a new problem: Chiri. Never yet had the big dog ridden a water-borne craft of any description. Chiri trusted only his own powers, and never depended on anything else. Persuading him to come along would not be the least of the problems they had to solve. Link stepped down on the raft and called him.

To his surprise, Chiri scrambled down the bank and walked unhesitatingly out on the raft. Link caught up a pushing pole, and shoved out from the bank. As soon as the raft moved, Chiri leaped back to shore. Link scratched his head. Obviously Chiri had no intention of taking the river ride; he had been willing to get on the raft only when it was resting against the bank. Well, that problem could be solved when the time came.

Link checked his waterproof match box, and filled it from the supply in his pack. Then he heated a chunk of venison fat, and when it was pliable he rubbed it on the head of every match that would not fit in the box. Every match was precious. None could be replaced, and coating them with tallow rendered them waterproof. Link handed a dozen matches to Antray.

"Just keep 'em in your pocket. If you have to take a swim on the way down, the matches will light when you get out of the water."

"Thoughtful of you," Antray said.

Link stole a sidewise glance at him. Beyond a doubt Antray appreciated the fact that the raft might capsize and throw both of them into the river, but he refused to worry about such a possibility.

Link unravelled a bit of the rope they had used as an anchor tie and bound his rifle and sleeping bag securely to the raft. He tied the axe and hunting knife beside them. The raft wouldn't sink. If the riders were thrown off, and survived, they could walk downstream and find it. When they did, they would again have the necessities for continuing their way of life, such as it was.

Inch by inch, missing nothing, Link inspected the raft and the articles he had tied to it. He could find no errors, nothing that needed improvement. When they were in swift water and he could change nothing anyway, he would probably think of a dozen things he should have done. He glanced at Antray.

"Looks shipshape to me, Admiral."

"I guess that's it, then."

Link felt a mounting nervousness, and an increased tension. He looked at the sun, but it still lacked an hour to high noon and they could not start until at least an hour and a half after noon. The river would be at its highest then. Link controlled an impulse to start now, to do anything that might lead to action.

"Better pull yourself together, Link," said Antray.

"I'm all right."

"Sure, you're calm as a boy who's just broken a window and doesn't want his father to find it out.

This raft isn't much heavier than the test raft I launched, and that got as far as the canyon."

"What happened after that?"

"That's something we'll find out," Antray said calmly. "Even if it's as bad as you think, we can't do anything about it now. Don't worry about it."

Link stopped watching the sun, because now every minute that passed seemed like an hour. He lay down, pillowed his head on his hands, and tried to sleep. He could not. The sun showed noon, and Link nibbled at a bit of venison. Antray ate heartily, then stowed the rest of the venison in the pack. They put out the fire, and carried the pack down to the raft, where Link tied it securely. Chiri, keeping a wary eye on the pushing pole, wagged his tail at him.

"Chiri," Link called.

Still watching the pushing pole, Chiri stepped down onto the raft. He was not nervous as long as it remained still, but he did not trust it in motion. He paid no attention when Antray picked up his pole, but as soon as Link reached for his, Chiri sprang back to the bank.

"You'll have to tie him, Link," Antray said.

"Looks that way."

Link took the length of rope he had used as an anchor tie the night he and Antray spent on the raft, and climbed the bank with it. Chiri came willingly when called. Link tied the rope around his neck and led him back to the raft. He slipped the other end of the rope beneath one of the logs and tied it. Chiri sat down, not liking the situation but accepting it. Long ago, when Link first captured him, he had learned the futility of fighting a rope and he knew he could do nothing now. Link knelt beside him and scratched his ears.

"Take it easy," he said. "Everything's going to be all right."

Chiri wriggled close to Link and licked his face. Link continued to scratch his ears, and after a while Chiri became noticeably less anxious.

"Launch time!" Antray said eagerly.

Link's nervousness had gone. Thinking about any perilous undertaking, he decided, was much harder to bear than action itself. Chiri rose to his feet when Link stepped back to the river bank, and whined. Antray took his place at the far side of the raft, a pushing pole balanced in his hands. Link laid his pole where he could snatch it up easily, walked to the tree which served as a mooring post, and untied the rope.

As the knot came loose he grabbed the rope with both hands, feeling the imperative tug of the river. Even here, in one of its calmest places, the water was very swift and strong. Link coiled the rope as he walked toward the raft, stooped to snatch up his pushing pole, then gave a leap that carried him out onto the raft.

He braced one end of the pushing pole against the bank, and gave a mighty shove that sent them far out into the river. He balanced on one side of the raft as the hungry current seized them, searching the river ahead for rocks that might upset them and ready to fend off as soon as the first appeared.

"Look at Chiri!" Antray shouted above the roar.

Link stole a sidewise glance. Chiri stretched full length, head on his paws and eyes unblinking. There was no evidence of fear about him, and scarcely any uneasiness. Link returned his attention to the river.

He flexed his knees, standing loose-legged in order to cushion any shock that might come. His heart seemed to leap into his throat when the bottom of the raft grated over submerged rocks and hesitated a moment. The current swept it on.

They came to a snarling riffle that whirled them rapidly along. For one sickening moment Link saw, out of the corner of his eye, a spray-drenched boulder that seemed to loom directly under Antray's side. The raft lurched violently away from it, and Link relaxed. Antray had seen the boulder, and fended them off.

They seemed to be travelling over submerged rocks at express-train speed, but there was no jarring or scraping. The two extra inches of water were enough! The raft shot into a stretch of comparatively quiet water at the head of the canyon, and though he dared not take time to look, Link was aware of high granite walls on both sides, and of the fact that they shut out the sun. The canyon was noticeably colder than the open stretches had been. Then, for a way, the river was almost placid.

Link glanced to the left, and was amazed to see five mule deer standing on what seemed to be a vertical wall. The deer were still, heads up and ears cocked forward as they watched the raft shoot past. Link noted that they were headed down-river to-ward the canyon. It was then that he became aware of the roaring ahead.

It was a dull, booming sound, like a far-off, tremendous wind. Link sank his pushing pole des-perately, trying to steer the raft toward the side of the canyon upon which the deer had stood. But, though the water was not very swift here, it was deep. Link could not reach bottom. The pole, un-like an oar, had little effect on the water's surface; he could not move the raft or swerve it. They shot into swifter water.

The booming became louder, increasing in volume. Link risked a swift glance at Antray, and the little man looked toward him at the same second. He held up his hand in salute, and grinned. Link brought his pushing pole in, and threw himself prone on the raft. Fumbling in his pocket with the other hand, he brought the jackknife out, opened it, and cut the rope that bound Chiri. Link regained his feet, and picked up his pole again.

They had taken a gamble, one which they probably would lose. Only one thing, a cataract of considerable size, could roar in such a fashion. Judging by the sound, no craft could go over it and live. But they still must try. Link grasped his pushing pole with both hands.

The roar became stronger, a steady, unchanging din that drowned out all other sound and seemed to shut out all the rest of the world. Helpless in the river's swirling current, the raft rushed on. It rounded a bend.

Spray seemed to fill the canyon and hang like a cloud over it. Link could see nothing but spray, hear nothing but the rush of water. He thrust at what he thought was a boulder, and the raft spun around. For a space the day turned dark.

Then, miraculously, they shot out of the darkness into the bright sunlight. The water was gentle here, and the raft floated almost slowly. Link realized what had happened. Instead of going over a falls they had passed under one, another cataract that dropped from a cliff into the canyon. Link glanced sidewise, and grinned happily as he saw Antray still on his side of the raft. Antray's lips moved, but all Link heard was the booming of the falls. It seemed as if he would never forget it. Antray tried again, and this time Link heard him.

"Look at Chiri."

The big dog was sitting in the center of the raft, ears alert and mouth open. He was looking at the river ahead, as if he hoped for another cataract to ride beneath.

A summer sun fell gently over everything when Link Stevens, Trigg Antray, and Chiri got back to Link's cabin on the Gander. A dog at the cabin announced their arrival with a series of sharp barks, and Link recognized Lud. Four pack horses grazed in the meadow along the river. A man came out of the cabin to look at them, then another man appeared beside him.

"Hello, John," Link said. "Hello, Hi."

For a moment the two men stared at the bearded, ragged travellers, then John Murdock gave a shout.

"Link!"

"Sure. Who'd you expect, Santa Claus? Meet a good friend of mine, Trigg Antray."

"Pardon my appearance, gentlemen," Antray murmured. "But I'm glad to see you. I really am."

John Murdock shook his head in amazement. "You got back!"

"Two of us did. Tom Garridge was killed by a cougar. You can put that in your official report."

"Come on in!" the constable roared. "Come on in and eat!"

Chiri walked over to renew acquaintance with Lud. Hi Macklin and John Murdock crowded Link and Antray into the cabin. Hi busied himself at the stove, while John Murdock tore open a parcel of dried peaches, and laid it on the table. Link grabbed some and stuffed them in his mouth.

"Umm! Good! Have another handful, Trigg."

"I already have both hands full."

Hi Macklin put his flapjacks and a huge pot of steaming coffee on the table. Link and Antray ate, and between bites tried to tell all that had happened. Hi Macklin's and John Murdock's eyes reflected their interest and envy, as Link concluded with the wild ride down the river.

"It flows right into the Goose," he finished. "Our raft's tied up within a half mile of where I crossed on the way in. But I know now how to get back into the Caribous. There has to be a path on the north side of the canyon wall, because I saw five mule deer coming down it. All you have to do is find the path."

"Looks like you've got a winter's job," observed Murdock. "Everybody in Masland will want to hear this."

"You tell 'em, then. I'm not going back to Masland."

"You're not!"

"Uh-uh. Did you bring grub and stuff in?"

"A big supply. I also got your rifle fixed, and plenty of ammunition for it."

Link grinned across the table. "You'll have to take Antray back. When the plane crashed he got his gizzard mixed up with his stomach, or something like that. He has to see a doctor, but don't keep him too long. I want him to meet me here before freeze-up. He's got some white moose, some caves, and nine bushels of ideas about the human race, that he wants to investigate. As for me, there's some wonderful trapping in the Caribous. I'll have to hump myself if I'm going to get everything packed in, a cabin built, and be back here in time to meet Trigg."

Link rose, grabbed another handful of dried peaches, and moved toward the door.

"I'll go see if Lud's too fat and lazy to pack."

ABOUT THE AUTHOR

JIM KJELGAARD's first book was *Forest Patrol* (1941), based on the wilderness experiences of himself and his brother, a forest ranger. Since then he has written many others—all of them concerned with the out-of-doors. *Big Red*, *Irish Red*, and *Outlaw Red* are dog stories about Irish setters. *Kalak of the Ice* (a polar bear) and *Chip, the Dam Builder* (a beaver) are wild-animal stories. *Snow Dog* and *Wild Trek* describe the adventures of a trapper and his half-wild dog. *Haunt Fox* is the story both of a fox and of the dog and boy who trailed him; and *Stormy* is concerned with a wildfowl retriever and his young owner. *Fire-Hunter* is a story about prehistoric man; *Boomerang Hunter* about the equally primitive Australian aborigine. *Rebel Siege* and *Buckskin Brigade* are tales of American frontiersmen, and *Wolf Brother* presents the Indian side of "the winning of the west." The cougar-hunting *Lion Hound* and the greyhound story, *Desert Dog*, are laid in the present-day Southwest. *A Nose for Trouble* and *Trailing Trouble* are adventure mysteries centered around a game warden and his man-hunting bloodhound. The same game warden also appears in *Wildlife Cameraman* and *Hidden Trail*, stories about a young nature photographer and his dog.

JIM KJELGAARD

In these adventure stories, Jim Kjelgaard shows us the special world of animals, the wilderness, and the bonds between men and dogs. *Irish Red* and *Outlaw Red* are stories about two champion Irish setters. *Snow Dog* shows what happens when a half-wild dog crosses paths with a trapper. The cougar-hunting *Lion Hound* and the greyhound story *Desert Dog* take place in our present-day Southwest. And, *Stormy* is an extraordinary story of a boy and his devoted dog. You'll want to read all these exciting books.

☐	15456	A NOSE FOR TROUBLE	$2.50
☐	15368	HAUNT FOX	$2.25
☐	15434	BIG RED	$2.95
☐	15324	DESERT DOG	$2.50
☐	15286	IRISH RED: SON OF BIG RED	$2.50
☐	15427	LION HOUND	$2.95
☐	15339	OUTLAW RED	$2.50
☐	15365	SNOW DOG	$2.50
☐	15388	STORMY	$2.50
☐	15466	WILD TREK	$2.75

Prices and availability subject to change without notice.

FROM THE SPOOKY, EERIE PEN OF JOHN BELLAIRS . . .

☐ **THE CURSE OF THE**   15540/$2.95
BLUE FIGURINE

Johnny Dixon knows a lot about ancient Egypt and curses and evil spirits—but when he finds the blue figurine, he actually "sees" a frightening, super-natural world. Even his friend Professor Childermass can't help him!

☐ **THE MUMMY, THE WILL**   15498/$2.75
AND THE CRYPT

For months Johnny has been working on a riddle that would lead to a $10,000 reward. Feeling certain that the money is hidden somewhere in the house of a dead man, Johnny goes into his house where a bolt of lightning reveals to him that the house is not quite deserted . . .

☐ **THE SPELL OF THE**   15357/$2.50
SORCERER'S SKULL

Johnny Dixon is back, but this time he's not teamed up with Dr. Childermass. That's because his friend, the Professor, has disappeared!

Shop at home
for quality childrens books
and save money, too.

Now you can order books for the whole family from Bantam's latest listing of hundreds of titles including many fine children's books. *And* this special offer gives you an opportunity to purchase a Bantam book for only 50¢. Here's how:

By ordering any five books at the regular price per order, you can also choose any other single book listed (up to $4.95 value) for just 50¢. Some restrictions do apply, so for further details send for Bantam's listing of titles today.